TOM BODETT

Williwaw!

A Dell Yearling Book

Published by
Dell Yearling
an imprint of
Random House Children's Books
a division of Random House, Inc.
1540 Broadway
New York, New York 10036

Visit us on the Web! www.randomhouse.com/kids

**Educators and librarians, for a variety of teaching tools, visit us at
www.randomhouse.com/teachers**

ISBN: 0-375-80687-3

Reprinted by arrangement with Alfred A. Knopf,
a division of Random House, Inc.

Printed in the United States of America

October 2000

10 9 8

OPM

To Courtney
With love, your dad

Thanks

To Jeff Dwyer and Elizabeth O'Grady for bringing me to the attention of Knopf Books for Young Readers. To Raphael Sagalyn for fifteen years of friendship and good advice. To Andrea Cascardi for her expert guidance and editorial instincts throughout the birth of this story, even as she nurtured one of her own.

Much appreciation goes to my oblong circle of companion writers, Kim Cornwall, Wendy Erd, Joel Gay, Tom Kizzia, Nancy Lord, John Rate, and Karen Wessel, for their wise and gentle counsel, and steadfast support. And, as always, to Gary Thomas and Luana Stovel for all the years of love and support.

Thanks most especially to Rita Ramirez, my wife and my partner in everything, including this story—which is at least half hers. And to my son, Courtney, who told me the only thing that would get a kid out into a storm like this was the hope of seeing his dad.

Williwaw!

CHAPTER 1

Ivan Crane and his sister September stood on their dock in the early morning Alaska chill of Steamer Cove. The big wind of the night before had taken a few more clinging yellowed leaves from the birch and alder trees scattered through the deep green forest of spruce. The white gleam of their radio antenna flashed in the very top of the tallest tree.

A pair of jet-black ravens glided overhead making their curious *kadok-kadok* sounds like water dripping into a bucket. Two loons drifted quietly together along the shore toward Mr. Berger's cabin across the quiet cove. The sun rose in the east as it did every morning, and Ivan and September argued as they did on most of them.

"Red sky at night, the sailors delight," Ivan insisted.

"No way!" September pounded a heel of her rubber boot on the wobbly dock so that it shuddered under their feet. "Dad always says, 'Red sky at night, the sailors *take flight*. Red sky in the morning, the sailors' hearts warming.' "

Ivan shook his head. "There was no red in the sky last night, and it blew like crazy. It's 'Red sky in the morning, the sailors

1

take warning.' " He turned toward the blushing sunrise partly to hide his enjoyment of tormenting his older sister and partly because he could hear the faint *blump-blump-blump* of the mail boat *Williwaw* throbbing through the still water. As always, Harry was right on time, about to round the point into the cove for his regular Friday visit.

"Harry can tell us. He's a sailor," September said.

"All Harry does is run an old wooden boat and read my comic books." Ivan waved away the notion that Harry could know anything, then added, "Dad will tell us himself because I bet he's on the boat too."

Ivan regretted the words as soon as he'd said them and jammed his hands down into the pockets of his wool coat. Although their father did often surprise them by returning early from his regular fishing trips, Ivan and September had made a pact never to bet or guess when he would come home. It was easy to jinx things like that. Never wave a ship out of sight, and never wager on its safe return, Dad always said.

The *Williwaw* heaved around the ugly pile of boulders lining the entrance to their cove. Confidently guiding his boat through the narrow channel with one hand, Harry waved his other big paw from the pilothouse.

"I'm sorry, Sep," Ivan said as if he'd somehow caused their father to vanish from the deck of the approaching boat.

September put her arm on her brother's shoulder. "It's okay. I was hoping for the same thing."

Their dad wasn't due home from his latest trip until the following day. He'd been gone the whole week this time—fishing for king crab out in the far-western waters of Alaska. It promised to be a good bonus to what had already been a terrific fishing season. The salmon runs had been strong all summer, and the catch sold for a good price. Now the seafood buyers were paying top dollar for king crab too. Although reduced to the lesser role of a crew member since the sinking of his own boat, their father had told the kids that if things kept going this well they could expect to build another by next year.

All through the seven years since their mother had died their father had insisted the new family fishing boat would be named the *Mrs Crane* in her memory. In that way they could all be together again. The thought of this arrangement filled Ivan and September with a homesickness that wouldn't settle even while they were at home. Every passing day without their dad seemed longer than the one before.

Harry, the smiling mail-boat skipper, might have read the disappointment on their faces. As the *Williwaw* pulled alongside the dock he put an extra push into his big voice. "Hello there, Captain. And how's the Little Miss this fine day?"

September groaned. She said nothing as she caught the line Harry tossed across the railing and bent to wrap it around the dock cleat. Harry had been calling Ivan "Captain" and September "Little Miss" for as long as she could remember. Ivan didn't much care one way or the other about being promoted to Captain, but September had never liked being a Little Miss. The older she became the less she liked it still; now that she was thirteen, it was intolerable. To exact her revenge, September called the large, furry mail-boat skipper "Big and Hairy" every chance she had. To his face, though, it was just plain "Hairy."

"We're fine this fine day, *Hairy*." September looked at her brother, who smiled at their private joke.

"An' you look fine—you look fine, Little Miss." Harry's teeth flashed like an anchor light out of the tangle of black beard and pieces of his breakfast. He stooped to fetch the neatly packed box of mail and supplies from under the hatch cover.

Harry *was* hairy. His dark pelt burst from the collar of his red-checkered shirt and spilled out of his sleeves onto the backs of his hands. Whiskers and curls grew from his head and face in every unlikely direction. Their dad said Harry always wore those red-checkered shirts so he wouldn't be mistaken for a bear and shot dead.

Harry handed the box over to Ivan, who found what he was looking for right on top. He made a sour face at Harry—a bear who drove a boat and brought them mail and was forever reading Ivan's comic books.

"You've been reading these again!" Ivan shook the colorful collection of sci-fi comics in Harry's direction.

The skipper only smiled. "Cover to cover! There's nothing to do on a mail boat so exciting as reading a comic book." Harry tossed his head back and blasted his huge goofy laugh, har har har! A laugh right out of a comic book itself, and so big it rang around the cove two or three times as Harry pointed a stubby black stovepipe of a finger at the comics.

"Tech Patrol from outer space! Saviors of the sonar system. Har har har! Going to rescue Earth from the attack of the four pied pipers! Har har har."

"It's *solar* system." Ivan shook his head. Harry never got it right. "And they're the *Four-Eyed Vipers*, not the four pied pipers. And don't tell me what happens. I've been waiting all month for these."

Harry laughed again and said, "You're lucky to have 'em at all. Some blow last night, warn't it? I was worried about you kids when I couldn't raise you on the box."

September gave her brother a cross look. "Ivan ran the radio battery down again playing that stupid pocket video game of his. We couldn't even listen to the news or weather this morning. How bad was it?"

"Bad enough, Little Miss. Came out of the north, so you were probably protected from the worst of it here. Port Vixen really got hit, though. Big blow. A williwaw tore through up there and capsized five boats."

September's insides stirred at the mention of williwaws: the dreaded fall windstorms like the one that drowned their mother and sank the family boat in the middle of Bag Bay on a powerful and sad night that lingered out on the very edge of her memory.

Harry seemed to remember as well and looked hard at both of them. "North winds are nothin' to fool with this time of year. You keep an eye on the weather and your ear to that radio before you go messin' out on the water, ya hear?"

September nodded obediently and turned to Ivan, who was already absorbed in his new reading material. "You better get that battery recharged before Dad calls tonight. Remember what he told us—if we can't stay in touch with him and Harry while he's gone, then it will be life on the farm with Aunt Nelda and Uncle Spitz from now on."

Even Harry cringed at the thought of Ivan and September's odd relatives who lived on an old broken homestead on the town side of Bag Bay and were far more odd than relative. Before anyone could say another word about that unpleasant proposal, they were interrupted by the sound of Mr. Berger's oars clunking against the other side of the *Williwaw*.

"It's bad enough an old man has to row his sorry self over for his own mail, but then he has to wait all morning to get it!" As if accusing Ivan and September, old Mr. Berger's permanently squeezed face peered over the boat. Harry spun around on the heels of his big rubber boots.

"You snuck right up on us, Berger. You better be careful or you're likely to give an old sailor a heart attack." Harry took an exaggerated breath of air and bent to gather up another small box of mail and supplies.

Mr. Berger, or ol' Mooseburger, as Ivan and September called their cranky and solitary neighbor, took the box without apology or thanks. "Well, you sure didn't sneak up on me. I seen this old tub comin' halfway across the bay through my eyeglass. Now you stand here flapping your yap at these wild children and leave an old man to fend for himself." Berger pulled the hood of his coat around his puckered features and sat down to his oars. "I've a mind to call the authorities on these thieving young weasels I got for neighbors."

September and Ivan were used to hearing this kind of talk from Mooseburger. He hated the Cranes. Actually, he hated everybody, but especially the Cranes—always did, and, it seemed, he always would. Ever since their dad and their mom

6

had settled on the land across Steamer Cove from Berger, the old man had made it his business to complain. He'd accused the kids of stealing from the time they were born. They had never stolen from Berger, but after having Steamer Cove to himself for more than thirty years, every fish, clam, berry, and drop of clear spring water seemed like personal property to him. He kept a telescope in his window and a keen eye on everything that went on.

Their dad told the kids to give Mooseburger plenty of room and to never—*ever*—give the old man any good reason to call in the authorities as he always threatened. "The last thing a struggling father and two kids living in the wilderness need is a bunch of nosy officials from town coming around," he'd said.

Some might not understand as well as Harry and a few others that a twelve-year-old boy and a thirteen-year-old girl were pretty well able to take care of themselves for a few days at a time while their dad went out to earn a living. These officials might think the kids would be better off across the bay with Aunt Nelda and Uncle Spitz instead of alone in their little log house in the woods.

"Good-bye, Mr. Berger. Have a nice day." September waved weakly to Berger's lowered head as he rowed away.

The old man only grunted with the next pull on the oars. Then Harry leaned over the railing and called after him. "Hey, Berger, did you hear on the news about the big blow up at Port Vixen last night? It was a real whopper! Williwaw, they say."

Berger looked up but didn't stop rowing. "I don't have a radio and you know it. If I wanted to hear from people I wouldn't live clear out here. Besides, I don't need no radio to tell me it's blowing outside when I got a tree falling down in my backyard."

Harry and the kids looked across the cove to Berger's place, and sure enough, behind the little house lay the gray trunk of a good-size spruce with the bright spot of a shattered stump shining white off to one side.

"I'll be darned." Harry scratched up under his cap. "You were lucky that didn't smash your house to bits. Ya need any help cuttin' that up?"

Berger pulled the oars and muttered as he moved away into the shadow of the standing timber, "I'll cut my own firewood just like I always have."

Harry turned back to Ivan and September and said with a wink, "I guess that means 'No, thank you.' You kids ought to steer clear of Mr. Berger until he cheers up."

"I'm not sure any of us will live that long," Ivan said darkly while he looked through the rest of their delivery. The box held the usual boring assemblage of general supplies. A jug of lamp oil and some wicks. Soap. A sack of flour, and one of brown rice.

"Yuck!" Ivan said, holding it away like a rotten fish. "We ordered white rice. I hate this stuff."

Harry shrugged. "I couldn't remember what you'd told me to get. It only said rice on my list. That's why I tried to hail you last night."

September nudged her younger brother with a knee. "See. I told you to put that stupid video game away."

"I know. I know! Dad doesn't call until tonight, and we don't leave the radio on all the time anyway. Jeez, Sep! I told you I'll recharge the battery today." Ivan shambled up the dock with only the comic books in his hands.

"And since it's my turn to cook, I'll fix you a nice bowl of brown rice for your troubles." September loved to pester Ivan about his video-game habit. He'd bought the game with his share of their money from selling clams at the Fourth of July picnic in town. Now that the days were getting shorter, it was all he wanted to do in the cabin during the long evenings. September felt left out of her thumb-twiddling brother's gyrations as he peered into his game to counterattack some imaginary invaders. She couldn't think of a single interesting thing to happen in their cove since video games invaded their lives. And she doubted anything of interest would happen as long as they were around. The two of them hadn't played cards by the lamplight or sat up telling ghost stories in months.

Thinking about the reality of another dull evening in the cabin with Ivan's glazed company, September pawed through the pile of mail in search of distraction. It was the usual stuff: bills, bulletins, catalogs, and some fishing journals.

Dull, dull, dull, dull, thought September until she turned up a fat manila envelope at the bottom. What she saw emblazoned across the front made her jump to her feet and call happily after her brother, "They're here, Ivan, they're finally here!"

Ivan sank about two inches into his boots as he read the big block letters clear from the end of the dock. ALASKA HOME-SCHOOL COURSE. "Oh please. Not already."

September danced the envelope around the narrow dock, singing wickedly. "School days, school days, dear old golden rule days."

Ivan tromped up the path toward the cabin, grumbling, "I think I'll go throw up."

Harry gunned the throttle on the *Williwaw*'s growling diesel, which didn't drown out his big laugh entirely. "Har har har. I'll leave you two scholars to your business. I've got my rounds to make."

He pulled the lines free of the dock and black smoke pumped from the stack as the old boat pulled away. "So long, Captain. Remember, watch your weather and stick close to that radio, Little Miss. If anything happened to you two while your father was away, he'd have my head."

CHAPTER 2

The long shadows of evening draped across the cove as Ivan aimed the front wheel of the motionless bike straight down toward the dock from the porch of the cabin. The chain and pedals made a low, whizzing sound. He gripped the handlebars tight and pumped like a champion.

"Low tide. The dock is floating at the ideal height. If I can get the speed up to critical velocity, I'll clear the water and land right on ol' Mooseburger's beach. He'll be so scared he won't have the courage to say a word about it, or ever bother us again. Okay, here goes…on three—one and two and—"

"Ivan, that's enough! You'll overcharge the battery!" September stood in front of her brother, wagging her hands back and forth to get his attention. "And it's time to eat, too."

Ivan slowed down his frantic pace and sat up on the stationary bicycle their father had rigged to drive the generator. The battery, when used exclusively for their VHF marine radio and broadcast receiver, only needed charging every week or so. But since Ivan had figured out his video game ran on the same voltage as the radio, and started jump-wiring the connections, it needed charging much more often. To fill the time during his long, boring ride to nowhere, Ivan would dream up amazing feats. He'd made the mistake of telling his sister about it.

"So what was it this time?" September smirked while she clicked the VHF to standby. "Vaulting over the Grand Canyon? Or were you terrorizing ol' Mooseburger again?"

"Mooseburger," Ivan said blandly, not wanting to give his sister the pleasure of annoying him. He climbed off the contraption and headed into the cabin. "Eww. Brown rice!"

"I told you," September said, grabbing the steaming dish from the stove top. "Besides, it's good for you."

Ivan plopped down in his chair and leaned unhappily on the table. "Who told you that?"

September thought a moment. "I guess Mom did."

"Oh." Ivan spooned some rice onto a plate and got quiet. He didn't remember as much about their mother as September did, and it bothered him sometimes. "Well, it still tastes bad."

"Don't you know that everything that tastes bad is good for you?" September tried to make a joke to move the subject in a new direction.

"You think skunk cabbage is good for you? How about baneberry?"

Leave it to Ivan, thought September, and was about to rise to the silly argument, when their VHF radio crackled across the kitchen.

"Steamer Cove, Steamer Cove, this is WFX98 Marine Operator with your call. Are you there, kids?"

Ivan leaped at the microphone before September could get out of her seat.

"Yeah, we're here!" he blurted into the mike, and then remembered his radio courtesy. "I mean, *roger*, this is WBN6408 Steamer Cove. Go ahead."

"Roger, Steamer Cove. I got your dad on the line. Stand by, please."

There were a few moments of empty static and then the welcome sound of their father's voice turned the simple cold black box of a radio into the warmest place on Bag Bay. "Hey there, you two wild cards!"

Ivan and September could hear the hiss of the distance and the clanking of machinery between their father's words.

"Hi, Dad!" the kids said together, and September continued in a hopeful voice, "Where are you?"

"I'm at the cannery in Dutch." Their dad sounded apologetic, and the kids knew why. "Dutch" meant Dutch Harbor, which was way out west in the Aleutian Islands and closer to Siberia than it was to Steamer Cove. They pictured him standing in the noisy din of a cannery wharf talking too loudly into a pay phone with the call being relayed by the marine operator in Kodiak to the little black radio in their kitchen.

"I thought you were coming home tomorrow." Ivan tried not to whine, but he couldn't hide his disappointment.

"I know, Ivan. I was, but the crab are thick out here, and the skipper asked me to stay with the boat. He's raised my share to keep me on, and that's good news. But do you want to hear the *really* good news?"

While their father paused, Ivan and September said nothing. They simply keyed the microphone once—which was the radio

equivalent of a grunt and a nod meaning "Yes," or "I understand," or, as in this case, "Go ahead."

"It means we might have the money to build the *Mrs Crane*,
and I'll never have to be away from you this long again!"

Ivan held the mike and let the sound and depth of the miles
between them seep from the little speaker. Building the new boat
was the most important thing on the whole wide ocean, and the
kids knew that, but they were also aware that news this good
from their dad was usually followed by news about as bad.

September could guess what it could be but needed to hear
it. She took the mike from Ivan's hand. "How much longer will
you be gone, Dad?"

"Two weeks, Temmy. Two more weeks, I'm afraid."

September looked at Ivan and Ivan looked at the radio and
they both braced themselves for what they knew was coming
next.

"I'll call the rowboat to say you'll be over tomorrow." Their
father's voice sounded a little sad as he used their radio code
name for Aunt Nelda. They called their aunt "the rowboat" and
their rowboat "the *Aunt Nelda*" because the small rowing dory
they used to get around inside the cove was, according to their
dad, a little *dinghy* and a little broad in the bottom.

He didn't like Aunt Nelda much more than the kids did, and
nobody liked Uncle Fritz—harmless, but a bore and universally
known as Uncle *Spitz* because he chewed tobacco and was always
doing just that. Mr. Crane had reluctantly and sporadically
called upon the aging couple to look after the kids in the years
since the death of their mother.

Aunt Nelda wasn't really their aunt. She was a cousin of their dead mother's who'd settled a long time ago on a homestead a few miles outside of town with her husband Fritz. They were modern-day pioneers and farmers, but to Ivan and September all they were was dirty and dull. They had goats who butted and stank and pigs that just lay around and stank. They kept a funny old broken-down horse that was so stiff and tired it sometimes blew over in the wind and couldn't right itself again. Uncle Spitz read about more seeds than he planted and talked endlessly about the low price of timothy and hay as an excuse not to grow any of it. Aunt Nelda seemed fixed to her chair and only pushed her nose above the windowsill high enough to check if the kids were doing all the chores she assigned. The kids would rather have gone to prison than to Aunt Nelda's farm, and they said so loudly and often.

"Please, Daddy. Not again." September didn't need to exaggerate her disappointment, and she could see her brother's face also falling. "We'll be okay here. Harry can look in on us."

"I don't think so, Temmy. Two more weeks is too long for you to be out there alone."

The words themselves sounded final, but Ivan and September heard a note of indecision in their dad's voice. Both kids knew their father resorted to Aunt Nelda only in the most extreme cases, as he had done the previous year when he was gone for a whole month fishing black cod. They could always tell when he really meant final and when he was feeling mealy. September gripped the mike.

"If we go to town tomorrow we won't get the potatoes and

carrots out of the garden, and it's going to frost any day now. You should see the leaves, how yellow they are already." September took a breath but left her thumb on the mike button so her father could not interrupt. "And we don't have all the red salmon out of the smoker. We'll need to get that bagged and stored before we go or the bear might come, and you wanted us to can a batch of butter clams for your stews and the good clamming tides are all this week and…and…" She was losing momentum.

Ivan grabbed at the home-school papers, snatched the mike, and took over. "And guess what, Dad? Our home-school lessons came today." He shuffled through the papers for the first time, but talked as if he'd been reading them all day. "Level seven and eight study guides. We've got history and geography and algebra, and how are we going to study if we're waiting hand and foot on the rowboat, and…"

September leaned into the mike and finished for him. "And you can trust us, Dad. You know you can."

September released the mike button and the radio speaker made a scratchy question mark of a sound. Ivan waited to breathe. The static seemed to grow more intense, as if it were the radio making up its mind rather than the father on the other end of it.

"All right," their dad said almost too softly to hear. "All right, then. I know I can trust you, and I know Harry will look after you. Isn't that right, Harry?"

"Yes, indeed!" Harry chimed in, revealing himself to be eavesdropping on the radio channel.

The kids and their dad laughed and September, vibrating

with excitement, spoke next. "You won't be sorry, Dad. Everything will be perfect when you get back. Absolutely perfect."

"I know. I know it will be. But I have two conditions on this. Number one is that you stay off the bay completely. No trips to town until I get back. Harry can bring what you need. Right, Harry?"

Click.

Their dad went on. "I heard about that blow up at Port Vixen last night. Bad news. So, condition one—off the bay. The other condition concerns you, Ivan."

Ivan sat back in his chair while his dad continued.

"Under no circumstances whatsoever are you to hook that silly video game up to our radios."

Ivan looked shocked and then glared at his sister.

"Don't ask how I know. I just do. You're going to mess up something with that one day and then you won't have a radio. And if you don't have a radio to call for help when you need it, then you can't be out there by yourselves. And if you can't be out there by yourselves, you know what?"

"Aunt Nelda's," the kids said grimly to each other but not into the radio.

"That's right. So—do we have a deal?"

Ivan picked up the mike again. "Deal," he said, and passed it to September.

"Deal." She felt as good and as grown as ever in her life.

"Now tell me." Their dad's voice sounded relieved. "Tell me what you see out the window."

This was the game they played every time their dad called.

They would look out the cabin window and describe their little cove to the homesick fisherman.

September loved doing this. She sat up and looked at the faintly lit scene beyond the kitchen windowpane. Ivan slumped in his chair and gazed sadly at the lifeless video game on the counter, ignoring his sister's radio tour.

"I see our two loons out by the dock. It's so calm they look like four loons with their reflections. The tide is coming in and the *Aunt Nelda* is leaning into the dock piling." September then peered farther through the waning day to the end of the dock and saw their good wooden skiff, with the permit number AK40523 painted black on its white sides.

"There's a kingfisher sitting on the motor of the *Four-O-Five*, looking for its dinner, and past that I can see Mr. Berger's small light reflecting all the way across to our side."

At the mention of the ornery neighbor their dad broke in again, using their radio code for Mr. Berger. "Remember, don't let the ground meat spoil. The less we say about our deal the better. And you're starting to break up out here, Temmy. Tell me one more thing and then we better sign off."

Their dad's voice sounded clipped and distant through the growing interference. September spoke louder and more slowly. "It's almost dark and the sky in the west is red, nearly purple now." Then she was reminded. "Hey, Dad, how does that go? Is a red sky at night a good thing or a bad thing?"

"Oh...remember...your mother...said about that." Their dad's signal was gravelly and peppered with gaps. "It's 'Red...ky... at...ight, sailors...' "

The static washed over their father like a wave and left Ivan and September with the surf sounds of an untuned radio.

"Dad?" September quizzed the mike.

"Dad?" She tried again, then shrugged to Ivan and signed off. "We're WBN6408 Steamer Cove, and we're clear."

The operator's voice interrupted the static one last time. "WFX98 Marine Operator, Kodiak—clear and out."

September put the microphone back on its clip. "I guess last night's storm must be between us somewhere."

"I guess so," Ivan said, grinning slyly. "Two more weeks of freedom! No Aunt Nelda! No Uncle Spitz! No school!"

"Wait a minute, Little Mister." September just thought of that and smiled at her own cleverness as she lit the lamp on the table. "The Little Mister and the Little Miss have to start our schoolwork whether Dad is here or not, and we've got enough chores to keep us busy for *three* weeks. We'll be lucky to get it all done."

"I know, *boss*," Ivan said, rolling his eyes. "I can live without video games if it means we'll never have to stay at Aunt Nelda's again!"

"Never again!" They cheered and hopped around the kitchen rattling the pots and dishes on the shelves. Ivan landed in his chair and started joyfully shoveling brown rice into his mouth before he knew what he was doing.

"Eeyuck!" Ivan swallowed hard, and September pointed at him and started to laugh, and it had a sound to it they both knew well. It was the sound of a giggle fit, and even as September clapped a hand on her mouth to stop it, Ivan burst into his. Their shrieks pealed through the doorway and out across the cove, turning the heads of kingfisher and loon and one spoiling old Mooseburger peering through his telescope on the other shore.

"This is KBAG radio coming to you live all over the Bag Bay area this Friday night, and it is nine o'clock, time for a look at the community bulletin board…"

September curled in the blankets on her bed in the corner next to the wood stove. She read through the home-school packet again and half listened to the town radio station. This was her favorite kind of evening. Sitting around by the soft lamplight and crackling fire snug at home with the radio bringing the whole wide world to their small cabin. Sometimes it would be the BBC on the shortwave clear from the other side of the planet in London, or English language broadcasts from Moscow, or Beijing, China, or even just what was going on fourteen miles across the bay in town. All of it was exciting, or at least interesting, and the radio kept it all at a comfortable distance from September's cove.

Ivan sat at the table plowing through his new comic books for the tenth time. He hunched his thin shoulders over the table, and his posture formed the very picture of boredom. It had become clear to him in the last hour that life without video games was hardly worth living at all. He took no comfort from the radio either—blathering on endlessly about Russian ballet, the quality of eggs in China, stray horses in the road, dances at the school gym, the price of fish, and the cost of bad weather. But even this drivel was more interesting than his bleak existence in Steamer Cove.

"Port Vixen is still cleaning up after the williwaw that pounded the small coastal community on Thursday night. Five fishing boats were lost and three badly damaged when the sudden gust tore the vessels from their moorings. Coast Guard spokesman Lieutenant J.G. Mayhee said there were no injuries and credits that good fortune to the cautious actions on the part of the residents.

"These people know their weather, and when that norther blew in they hunkered down on shore and let the boats fend for themselves.

"That's News. And remember, the community bulletin board is brought to you by the Dockside Traders—general store, snack bar, and game arcade, featuring the exciting new video sensation: Tech Patrol and the Invasion of the Four-Eyed Vipers."

"Oh, man!" Ivan grabbed his head with both hands. "This is torture! They've got the new Tech Patrol game in town, and we have to stay here where I can't even play my lame little pocket game! Two weeks without video! It's not fair."

"It's fair," September said sleepily from her pile of blankets. "It's just no fun."

Ivan ground his teeth. "I wish you'd stop repeating everything Dad always says. It's bad enough the first time." Ivan looked over his shoulder and could see only the blond top of his sister's head already on her pillow with the home-school package stacked on the shelf above.

"Are you going to sleep, Sep?" he asked.

"Umm-hmm," the blankets said.

Ivan looked at his pocket video game lying dead on the table, then over at the green glow of the radio dial. "Good night, Sep."

"Hmm," she said over the beginning of the evening music program.

Ivan tapped his finger along with a dull waltz while he counted to a hundred.

"Sep?"

"Mm?"

"Sep-tem-ber?" he sang.

The wood gave up a little pop in the cook stove and Ivan slid from his chair.

As his sister breathed to the slow, lilting music, Ivan reached behind the radio sets and stealthily pulled the tangle of wires into the light.

He'd done this dozens of times over the summer. Once he'd discovered he could run his new pocket video on the same low-voltage converter as the two radios, he found a way to rig it directly above the converter between the radios and the big boat battery their dad had wired to the generator bike. Ivan knew the price of batteries, and it didn't take too many days with the new video game to see he wouldn't be able to afford his habit for long. Every night was another three dollars' worth of double-A batteries, plus gas for the outboard because the nearest battery store happened to be a cold fourteen-mile skiff ride away.

Ivan had also discovered long ago that he had a knack for cobbling together old flashlight parts and stray bulbs into working lamps. He knew the value of a flashlight in a life without electrical power, and his dad had always encouraged him to make the most of what was at hand.

So with one measure inspiration and two measures desperation Ivan had fashioned a way to hot-wire his game into the radios. It was a simple matter of taking some of the old flashlight parts and wire scraps and twisting them around the battery pack on both ends. He'd used his pocketknife to scrape some places on the radio wires to clip onto. He had spent many a late summer's evening since then blasting electronic bad guys with his two thumbs.

Ivan never rigged the radios when his dad was around, and as he tried to do it now in the dim light of the oil lantern, he couldn't imagine how his father had found out. He raised his head to check that September was still sleeping. She wouldn't have told. They always kept each other's secrets, no matter how mad they sometimes were at each other.

Ivan's fingers searched for the scraped places on the wires. He found the first and carefully twisted his hot wire around it. He couldn't see how the voltage converter was lying, but felt around some more to be sure it was all clear of the bare leads tied to the big battery. All the wires seemed clear of each other. He felt another scraped place and quickly turned his loose wire around it.

That's that, Ivan thought joyfully as he heard the pocket game booting up. He lifted his head in time to see the green glow of the radio receiver dial turn a bright yellow. The music suddenly got louder, too. Weird, he thought, and clutched at the volume knob before the music could wake his sister. The marine radio let out a heated moan. By the time Ivan got his hands over the speaker it had already gone quiet with a long pitiful whizzing sound. Then the music quit altogether and the dial of the receiver, along with Ivan's joy, slowly faded to black.

He sucked in his growing panic and tried the video game. Also dead in his hands. He reached clumsily behind the radio again to check his connections. As soon as he did he heard a sound like a sparkler and saw a little whiff of gray smoke float to the ceiling reeking of burned plastic and death.

Uh-oh.

September woke up. "Ivan? What's that smell?"

"What smell?" Ivan slid his video game back into the shadows.

"It smells like burned wax, or a pot handle. Are you cooking?"

Ivan took the offer. "Umm, yeah. I was cooking a candle. I mean, I set a candle down by the stove."

September laid her head back down. "Well, you better clean it up. And turn the music back on, would you? It helps me sleep."

"Sure, Sep. Sleep tight."

Oh man oh man oh man. Ivan tried the radio knob—*click, click, click*—nothing. No sound. No light. He reached for the wires again. They were hot. A piece of melted plastic coating stuck to his finger.

"Oww!"

September was up. "What are you doing, and where is my music?"

Pulling the burned finger from his mouth, Ivan caved. "Oh, Sep, I think I've really done it this time."

"Done what?" September heard the terror in her brother's voice. She put both feet on the floor.

"I think I fried the radio. *Both* radios!" Ivan's eyes puddled up.

September padded across the room in her bare feet and leaned over the quiet radio sets. Dragging the video game into view with its scorched dangling wires, she turned and stood looming over her brother.

"Ivan Crane! What were you thinking?"

Ivan cowered. "I don't know what happened. It always worked before."

"Oh, cut it out!" September dropped the game on the table. "You fixed a flashlight once and now you think you're Thomas Edison. And that's not even the point! This is exactly what Dad said *not* to do."

"He's going to kill me, isn't he?"

"Worse than that." September was starting to sound more sick than angry. "He's going to send us both to the rowboat farm."

Ivan's tears flowed freely and reflected in the lantern, making fiery streaks down his face. September thought he looked so broken he might die before anybody got the pleasure of killing him.

Ivan suddenly rallied. Wiping his tears with the stroke of a sleeve and seeming to forget them just as quickly, he said, "Nothing will happen if Dad doesn't know."

Just the sound of it drained some of the heat out of the room. September took a small step backward. "What are you saying?"

"I'm saying nobody has to know I fried the radios if we get

25

them fixed before Dad's call next Friday." Ivan's eyes darted to the coffee can above his bed on the other side of the stove. "I have almost twenty dollars left from selling clams on the Fourth. It won't cost more than that to fix a few burned wires."

Ivan spilled the can of loose bills and change onto his blanket. "See? All we gotta do is take the radios to the repair shop in town, and nobody has to know."

September shook her head. "That's the only other thing Dad told us not to do."

"But it's an emergency!" Ivan pleaded.

"It's *your* emergency. I was asleep when this happened." September turned her back to her brother and looked at her reflection framed in the black window. Ivan appeared in the glass beside her—a slightly shorter version of herself with cropped hair sticking up every possible way rather than long hair that hung down every possible way.

Ivan folded his arms to match his sister's. "It's my fault, but it's our problem. Dad isn't going to send just one of us to the farm."

September stayed quiet for a moment. A piece of resolve washed away with the gurgle of the tide coming through the barrier rocks of the cove.

"It's not honest," she said for the record.

"I know."

"It's risky." She still didn't move.

"Could be." Ivan chanced a look sideways.

September thought some more and said, "But it sure beats feeding the pigs at Aunt Nelda's."

"No doubt." Ivan struggled to keep a serious face.

"Well then," she said, trying unsuccessfully to keep a smile from pushing the frown from her own face. "I guess we better get to town in the morning and get it over with."

CHAPTER 3

Brilliant and unpredictable, September, the month, required a lot of attention. September, the girl, was giving it all of hers as she faced the Popsicle-red morning sky. She wiggled inside her oversize wool coat and stomped her feet on the frosty dock planks to stop the chill shivering up her back.

The month of her namesake held a confusion of beauty and peril for September. Her mother had named her for the most mixed-up month of them all. The September of the cold mornings and the warm afternoons. The hot-pink meadows of fireweed turned blood color while birch and cottonwood trees leaped like orange and yellow fires from dark spruce forests.

Nothing in September stayed the same for long. The water on the bay could be flat and shiny as a plate in the morning and then be agitating like a washing machine by lunch. September studied the peaceful cove and calm bay while a lazy breeze brushed her face. *A south wind mumbles warm and low.*

Whenever a memory of her mother struck September, a blend of joy and loneliness came with it. The scenes in September's head were clear as the morning air.

The east wind blows you side to side…

Their mother would sing and rock September and Ivan back and forth on her knees.

The west wind makes like a ride on a slide…

Down her legs they would go.

A south wind mumbles warm and low…

She'd swoop down and grumble into their necks while they shrieked with glee.

And the north wind blows you all the way home.

To me! she'd say, gathering them up close in her arms.

"What's that you say, Sep?" Ivan trudged down the dock lugging a red gas can in each hand.

September hadn't realized she was speaking out loud and hugged her arms around herself, a little embarrassed. "Nothing. I was just thinking about Mom."

"I was too," Ivan said, setting down the heavy containers. "It must be the weather. As I was filling the gas cans, that old rhyme kept running through my head."

"The 'Four Winds' song," September said, not surprised. "It must be the good weather."

She looked out at the smooth bay, then bent to load one of the cans. "We couldn't have picked a better day to go to town, even if it is the last thing in the world we're supposed to be doing. What would Dad say if he saw us?"

Ivan imitated their father's angry face and low voice. "I'm so disappointed, Ivan. September, I expected better than this from you."

The truth of what he said was lost in the fun of it. Still chuckling, September made a place among the loose buckets and tools and put the can in the bottom of the *Four-O-Five*.

Ivan handed down the other can and said, "This is the last of the gas from the fuel drum. We better buy more to replace it or Dad's going to wonder where it all went." He picked up the cardboard box containing the two broken radios and the video game packed carefully in plastic bags and clean rags.

September took the box and gently set it on the rear seat. "Do you really think we'll have enough money after we fix these?"

"Oh, sure," Ivan boasted. Twenty dollars seemed like a lot of money, and he had no doubts that it would fix any number of radios and video games, fill a gas can, and buy them each a chocolate shake to boot. "Don't you worry, Sep," he said, and grandly patted his pants pocket. "The captain has the funds for the fun."

"Oh, great. First you're Thomas Edison, now you're Bill Gates." September pumped the primer bulb on the fuel line to the outboard. "Don't forget, Little Mister, you owe me big for this. The first chocolate shake belongs to me. Even if it's the *only* one."

Ivan said nothing as their attention was drawn to the sound of a skiff beyond the entrance to the cove. A sleek boat sped up to the jagged rocks and turned sharply away again. Hoots and peals of laughter came from the group on board as it roared out of sight.

"Crazy townies looking for a clam beach," September said as she wrapped her fist around the starter cord. "They weren't even wearing life jackets."

Ivan scowled, but whatever he said was lost in the growl of

the motor coughing to life in a cloud of blue smoke. While the engine warmed up, the kids struggled into their rubber rain gear and cinched their hoods down tight around their faces. No matter what the month, the long ride to town was a cool one, and the rubber coats would break the wind.

September pulled her big orange life vest over the bulk of her clothes, then helped Ivan on with his. Just as town kids wouldn't hesitate about fastening their seat belts in a car, the Crane kids couldn't imagine leaving the cove without putting on a life jacket. They'd been taught to respect the deadly cold water that surrounded their lives on Bag Bay. As peaceful as it often looked, life expectancy in those frigid waters was measured in minutes without some kind of flotation—and then maybe only an hour with that.

As Ivan pushed the *Four-O-Five* away from the dock, September dropped the motor into gear and swung the bow out toward open water. She twisted the throttle, urging them into the strong tidal current pouring through the narrow channel to their little cove. They heard the sound of water rushing like a river around the rocks September avoided as she steered them safely through the passage. No wonder those townies turned around, she thought smugly. They probably couldn't even see the way in. September and Ivan had been handling this skiff even longer than they'd been doing home school. They'd navigated the bay, with and without their dad, so many times they hardly noticed it anymore. Ivan hunkered down in the point of the bow partly to stay out of the wind and partly to keep the front end weighted down and steady. The motor roared, making conversation difficult.

September held the tiller on the motor with a gloved hand and steered. There was no sign of the other boat, and she figured they must have gone into the neighboring Huckleberry Cove to dig for steamer clams. Fair-weather weekends like this often brought town people out their way, but otherwise the town across the bay stayed an hour boat ride and one entire world away from Steamer Cove.

September thought about the community she lived so close to and felt such distance from. Kids on bikes cruised down the street free as gulls instead of being wired to their father's battery banks. They had moms in cars who drove them places in their perfect clothes that smelled of soap. They didn't bounce around in work-skiffs speckled with fish scales and jam dumpy rubber boots on their feet. Town kids wore expensive athletic shoes and could drink shakes every day as if they were nothing.

No matter how hard she worked at being clean, September knew she would never smell or look like a town kid, and a chocolate shake would always mean something. Her and Ivan's clothes were clean enough but scented with the rich earth smell of pure spring water. Their hair had a little bit of wood smoke in it from the sauna stove, and there was gas on their hands from handling the outboard motor. If town kids think that smells funny, then that's their problem, she thought.

Sure, they had stores in town, and candy, and magazines to ogle. But there was also dust and machinery roaring around pointlessly in the hands of frantic people. They lived in houses packed together in neat little rows like beehive boxes. Certain town kids thought that people who lived in the forest across the bay and didn't go to real school were some kind of freaks. "Bush rats," they called them under their breath. Or right out loud when there were enough of them to feel brave.

September grew angry by the thought, then checked their course to cast it from her mind. The fourteen miles of water to town was enough to put it over the horizon and out of sight. A compass had to be used for the first few miles, and then the town would begin springing up piece by piece. First the radio tower, then the school on the hill, the church steeple, the flag over the harbor, the loading crane at the sawmill, and so on until the whole thing rose before them like some magic garden that grew out of nothing.

That's exactly what it felt like to Ivan—magic. He peeked over the edge of the skiff, saw they were getting closer, and settled back down with a smile into a loose coil of line. Living in the bush was okay as far as he was concerned—just okay. He liked fishing and hunting, exploring the woods, getting to know all the animals, cruising in the boat, and all that. But it was all so *ordinary*. Nothing exciting like town where things were happening every way you turned. People watched color televisions in big soft living rooms instead of sitting around in the kitchen with their pathetic radios. There were more kinds of candy than he could remember, and those hot French fries and cold chocolate shakes at the Dockside Traders.

The Dockside. The very thought of it gave Ivan the feeling all was well in the world. No matter that they were crossing the bay against direct parental orders and risking a life of boredom and drudgery on Aunt Nelda's farm in order to repair two radios he shouldn't have been messing with in the first place. Inconvenient details such as these were no match for the charms of the Dockside Traders. There simply was nothing so bad that it couldn't be redeemed by a chocolate shake and a couple of dollars' worth of Tech Patrol.

Ivan sat up when September slowed the engine to a low groan at the entrance to the harbor. Looking around cautiously, he said, "Tie up over behind the harbor master's shack so nobody knows we're here. You go to the Dockside and wait while I run the radios up to the electronics shop. As soon as I get to the Dockside, we'll have our shakes and head for home."

"Nothing else," September said firmly, then looked across the harbor and saw the *Williwaw* in its usual spot across from the fuel dock. "And whatever you do, don't let Harry spot us," she warned.

No sooner had September spoken than they heard a muffled har har har lilting across the calm harbor from the old mail boat. There was no danger of Harry spotting them and September knew it.

"Hairy's watching cartoons again," she said as she turned in behind the harbor master's place and cut the engine. "You could drop a bomb out here on any Saturday morning and Harry would never know."

Just then a noise very much like a bomb thundered down the dock ramp above their heads. A kid in low-slung pants on a skateboard streaked along the dock and weaved his way out of sight among the bowsprits of the harbored fishing boats.

"Townies," September huffed.

"Cool!" Ivan marveled. He unbuckled his life vest and

dumped his rain gear in the bottom of the skiff. Bounding up the ramp, he called over his shoulder, "See you at the Dockside in ten."

September strolled casually up to the street and stopped for a look around before edging toward the Dockside Traders. Coming around the corner, she peered through the big window of the snack shop. She wasn't so worried about who might see her in town, but as always, in who she might have to see. The last thing she wanted was an encounter with some snotty town kids. The place appeared empty. She looked down at her muddy boots and breathed easier.

September wondered why she never noticed her clothes on the other side of the bay. The most thought she ever gave to clothing at the cove was to put on more if she felt cold. If she felt warm, she took some layers off. So how come something as simple as walking through the door of a snack shop made her feel like such a big dirty blond-haired slob? A set of nerve-rattling bells jangled on the opening door, and September realized she wasn't alone as soon as it closed behind her.

Over by the newspaper racks, two town girls giggled into the pages of their magazines. September, feeling trapped, quickly retreated to the corner table, as far away as she could get from them. She left her back to the room and felt the sound of the sniggering girls burning in her cheeks.

Hurry up, Ivan, she thought, nervously twisting her jacket sleeve and losing all appetite for chocolate shakes.

A shape passed outside the window and the door swung open in a hail of bells. Instead of the familiar form of her younger brother, there stood a boy she recognized to be the skateboarding daredevil from the harbor ramp. He tucked his flame-colored skateboard under his arm and screwed his backward cap down tighter on his shaggy head. His shoes squeaked on the tile as he loped by the first table and noticed September in the corner. He stopped and looked right at her. It seemed like a rude thing to do but somehow it didn't feel in any way insulting. He had a curious look on his face that asked "Who are you?" Which was a lot better than the "What are you?" she normally saw on townies' faces.

"Hi," he said with a big grin.

"Uh, hi," September almost choked.

"My name's TC."

September tried to dredge a voice out of her throat. Finally she managed, "I'm, umm, Sep—"

But it was too late. A burst of silliness came from the magazine section, and TC turned to the other kids. "Oh, hi, Sheri. Hi, Annette. I didn't see you there."

"Hi, TC," said one in a voice that ran like pancake syrup. TC started away from September's table as if he'd been hit in the back of his baggy pants with a stick.

September felt as if she were sitting in a pool of hot tar. Her voice was still caught in her throat, and though every cell and fiber in her body wanted to run for the street, she couldn't move. All she could do was fume while the town girls' hissing whispers filtered across the room.

September shrank when she heard TC's loud voice.

"Bush rats? What's that?"

The girls snapped silent when they saw September start to come around in her chair, so TC never heard whatever else they had to say. But apparently he'd heard enough because he was already walking straight toward her with his eyes wide.

"Wow!" he said, dropping the skateboard and falling into a chair. "Do you really live across the bay? Over there?" TC pointed beyond the blue water to the blur of dark trees and rock faces of the far shore hovering below the jagged mountain peaks.

"Yes," September said coldly, bracing for an insult.

It never came. "Awesome," he said, leaning forward, his eyes full of interest and his mouth twisted with questions. Just then Ivan clanged open the door and stopped, looking as sorry as dirt on a gum ball.

"Ivan, what's wrong?"

CHAPTER 4

Ivan glanced at his sister and at the strange kid, then down at the skateboard. He offered a thin-smiled hello without even coming all the way into the store. "We gotta go, Sep. Back to the skiff—now!"

September could hear the urgency in her brother's voice. "Bye," she said, and left TC at the table without so much as a look back. But she didn't leave too fast to miss TC's closing comment.

"Way cool," he said, and the door closed on a spray of cackles from the girls.

"Go, *go*," Ivan said, hauling his sister onto the boardwalk by her sleeve. "This way. Keep your head down."

September stopped and yanked her arm free. "Ivan Crane! Tell me what is going on with you!"

Ivan glanced nervously down Front Street along the harbor. "Do you want the bad news, the very bad news, or the worst news?"

"Let's start with the bad."

Ivan looked down the street again. "Aunt Nelda is in town and coming this way."

September got moving again. "Why didn't you say so?"

They headed toward the harbor to make their getaway. Ivan pulled out in front looking constantly over his shoulder at the street above. September noticed his empty hands.

"Where are the radios?"

"That's the very bad news," Ivan said, not even slowing. "The repair guy has to call Seattle to order some of the parts I cooked. So the sets won't be fixed until Thursday or Friday."

September reached out and grabbed her brother by the arm. "You mean we have to come back to town again?"

Ivan turned down the ramp to the dock with his sister clamped on to him. "That's not the worst news. The worst news is they took my twenty dollars for a deposit and we have to come up with another sixty for the whole repair. And worse than that—he said my video game is completely destroyed. Game over!"

September swung Ivan around to face her. "I couldn't care less about your stupid game. Where are we going to find sixty dollars by Thursday?" Her tone had the edges of despair in it. "We need those radios by the time Dad calls, or it's the farm!"

Ivan looked beyond his sister to Front Street. "Well, there she is. Maybe we should just go turn ourselves in now and get it over with."

September turned and saw Aunt Nelda heaving herself along the boardwalk, carrying a sagging burlap sack. "No way! Come on!"

They ducked down the dock toward their skiff and huddled behind the corner of the harbor master's shack. September peered out at Aunt Nelda, who continued on her way, huffing and muttering to herself. "What's she doing down here in town?"

Ivan stayed out of sight. "I saw her come out of the Bag Bay Fish Company with that sack. Probably buying salmon heads for that awful stew she makes."

September continued to watch until Aunt Nelda had trundled beyond the Dockside Traders. "No, I bet it's a bag of butter clams. She puts up gallons of clam chowder every fall. Dad says she's too fat to bend over and dig them for herself these days, so she buys them from the fish company."

Brother and sister saw the wheels turning in the other's head, and each had the same notion at nearly the same moment.

"Clams! That's it!" September cried.

"We'll sell clams to the fish company!"

The kids had spent long days digging bucket after bucket of clams with their father last fall. Once the salmon season wound down, the fish processors bought butter and steamer clams by the bag load from anyone who brought them in. At a dollar a pound, it was worth it to fishermen like their father to turn their attention to this enterprise for a little extra cash once the weather turned cold.

"Do you think we can dig sixty dollars' worth by Thursday?" Ivan jumped into the skiff and piled on his rain gear.

September eagerly found her way into hers and primed the gas line. "They don't call it Steamer Cove for nothing!" she said, and jerked the motor to life with the first pull.

Puttering through the quiet harbor, the kids kept a wary eye out for Aunt Nelda, Harry, or anyone else who might cause more trouble. September and Ivan saw TC come out to the boardwalk overlooking the harbor.

"Who was that kid?" Ivan asked, and just as he did TC lifted his hand and gave one big long wave as if he wasn't sure they saw him. Ivan waved back automatically. September steered them around the breakwater wall and cautiously raised her free hand before they left the harbor.

"TC. He seems a little strange," she said, gunning the throttle and urging the *Four-O-Five* out into the calm bay. "But nice," she added under the growl of the motor as the skiff found its speed and skimmed across the breeze-ruffled water toward home.

The fresh cool air across her face and the bright sun made September bunch her features into a half-smiled squint that became more smile than squint with every passing minute. She replayed with relish the look on the townies' faces when TC turned his back on them and plopped right down in front of her. *You really live across the bay? Over there?* He'd said it as if "Over there" were Magic Kingdom, Paradise Island, the White House, and Beverly Hills all rolled into one.

Steamer Cove—Adventureland! September laughed to herself. She realized that she was returning from town with a smile on her face for the first time in a long while. She looked back over her shoulder at the shrinking buildings on shore and imagined eyes upon her. *Look at them go. Over there!*

Yes, over there, she mused, with clams and chores for something to do, birds, bears, and Mooseburgers for company, and a luckless little brother for entertainment. September smiled at her luckless brother and dug a hand around in the toolbox at her feet for a tide book. They'd better not miss a single low tide if they were to raise the money by Thursday.

◆ ◆ ◆

Ivan sat with his back to the bow of the skiff, slowly turning miserable as the town vanished bit by bit over the horizon. Thoughts of chocolate shakes and Tech Patrol went with it, and the reality of their situation crept inside of him like the damp air making its way down his neck. He couldn't imagine how it might have gone any worse—they had no radios, no videos, no money. They didn't even get the gas can filled. It would be something on the order of a miracle, he figured, if their dad didn't find out about all of this.

Pulling his jacket collar tight, he huddled deeper into the boat and felt tired with the weight of the work ahead. Not only do we have to do every single chore we normally do, but now we have to dig sixty pounds of clams as well, he thought miserably. *Sixty pounds!* He wondered how many buckets' worth that was. They'd better not waste any time getting started.

He looked at September and could tell she was thinking about the same thing. Driving the boat with one hand, she clumsily leafed through the book of tide tables with the other.

"When's the next clam tide?" he shouted.

September moved a thumb down the wind-riffled little page. It took some complicated-looking columns of numbers to spell out the size and timing of some of the largest tidal activity in the world, but experience told her exactly where to look. "There's a minus two footer in the morning," she yelled, and jammed the book in a pocket.

Ivan nodded. While anxious to get at the business of making money, he knew the clams would make themselves available only when the tide allowed it. Unlike with sisters, there was no arguing with oceans.

Ivan's cranky mood made it all the way across the bay with them. They went straight to work on getting the fish out of the smoker, and not even the taste of a fresh batch of smoked red salmon cheered him up. Although they'd all be sick of it by Christmas, the first smokehouse fish of the fall always tasted best, and September was puzzled by her brother's lack of enthusiasm.

"It's sure good eating around here in September," she offered as they next dug into the garden.

"Same stuff, different day," Ivan fumed, plucking fat carrots from the soft dirt and dropping them in a basket. That morning's frost had commanded them to start canning the vegetables for storing in the root cellar. They spent the rest of the afternoon and into the evening dredging carrots, beets, and potatoes out by the armloads. The cabbages were brought in for sauerkraut, and the zucchinis would be pickles before the snow flew.

September rubbed the littlest, sweetest carrots on her pant leg and ate them on the spot. "Mmm," she purred, looking at the baskets overflowing with fresh produce.

"Ugh," Ivan grunted, looking at the same thing.

After a late dinner of boiled cabbage, potatoes, and carrots the kids read through their school papers in silence. September stole glances at her brother as he flipped his pages peevishly, and she decided to leave him alone. He'd had some bad news followed by a long, hard day. A good night's sleep is all he needs, she figured. She could use the rest herself with all the work that lay ahead. As much as September loved the work of living off the bounty of Steamer Cove, this week was going to be a challenge. By the time they were done with all the canning, the pantry shelves would be groaning with hundreds of jars of garden goods.

Ivan and September would be groaning right along with the shelves because between all the cooking and carrying and pumping the water from the spring box, they had wood to split, a new outhouse hole to dig, a leak to fix on the sauna roof, and the *Aunt Nelda's* bottom to paint. And in their spare time, as if they had any, there was sixty dollars' worth of clams to dig. Thanks to video-crazed brothers.

"That low tide is going to be awful early," she advised him as she snuffed the lantern at her bedside. Ivan continued to flip pages noisily at the table.

"What are you reading about?" she asked, trying one last time to get Ivan out of his head.

"Geography," he said.

"I love geography!" she bubbled. "Don't you?"

"No," he said flatly, and blew out his lamp.

The morning, thought September. He'll feel better about things in the morning.

CHAPTER 5

The tiny dory traced a crooked trail in the water. The morning sun seeped over the surrounding hills and nearly shone through the gray canopy. Not quite enough to leave shadows, but enough to warm the quiet air and raise a few hungry late season no-see-ums, a notoriously wicked gnat about which their father said, "You might not see-um, but you sure can feel-um." Ivan sat on the empty clam buckets and swatted absently at his ears while September pulled on the oars.

"Who you waving at?" September tried to raise her brother's spirits, which had not improved with a night's sleep, by repeating one of their dad's old jokes. Ivan ignored her and continued flapping at the bugs around his head.

The *Aunt Nelda*'s bottom scritched onto the pebbly beach. Ivan wobbled on his bucket and still said nothing. September was tired of this.

"Ivan Crane! You haven't said a word to me in a day!"

Wearing his rubber boots, Ivan stepped over the side and into the shallow water, hauling his bucket behind him. "Did too."

"When?" September sloshed up the beach with the bowline in her hand and uncoiled its length.

"This morning." Ivan set his bucket down in the gravel and looked at the clam squirts all around them. "This morning I said 'Get up.' "

"I didn't hear you. I was sleeping."

"Not after I said it you weren't." Ivan laid back his head and yawned. Two immature eagles circling overhead caught his attention. Their mottled young feathers poofed out, making them appear bigger than their sleek and famously marked parents. These were gigantic dark shapes against the thin cloud cover. The head of an adult bald eagle made a vivid white spot in a tree straight across the cove above their cabin. No doubt looking for scraps from the smokehouse, Ivan thought.

"I wish I were an eagle," he said quietly.

"If wishes were fishes we'd eat them." September cringed as soon as the words left her lips. It was another one of their father's endless collection of stupid things to say. Ivan hated when she repeated them, and she knew this was no way to get him talking again.

"Sorry. Bad habit." Bending to loop the bowline around a goose-size rock at her feet, she tried again. "What would you do if you were an eagle?"

"Fly away."

September looked up at the young birds drifting above the beach on the warm air currents. "Fly away where?"

"I don't know." Ivan stood up and pitched a stone hard at nothing. "I'd fly to town, or Seattle—anywhere but this hole in the woods." Ivan picked up another stone and jammed it right toward the *Aunt Nelda*, just missing. "Maybe I'd fly out to Dutch Harbor and sit on some fisherman's head and say, 'Hey, go pick your own carrots! Chop your own wood! Paint your own dumb dory!'"

Ivan let loose another stone at the little boat and zinged it right off the starboard side, leaving a chip in the paint they both could see from where they stood.

"Ivan! What are you doing?" September leaped the distance between them and screamed right in his face.

Ivan took a step backward and tripped over the clam bucket. He fell hard on his bottom, and the surprise and humiliation of it mixed up with his anger and brought tears to his eyes. September softened.

"Ivan, really, what is the matter?"

"What's the matter?" Ivan wiped a sleeve across his face and found his anger again. "You ask me what's the matter?"

Pushing aside his sister's helping hand, Ivan came to his feet and kicked a spray of stones down the beach. "This is what's the matter! We live in the middle of nowhere with nothing to do but work! Haul that water, Ivan! Chop that wood, son! You kids get busy now! And as soon as I decide to have some fun—pop goes the radios! Sixty pounds of clams, please! Can't you see it, Sep? This isn't a childhood. It's a labor camp!"

Silly as her brother sounded, September knew he was serious and tried to say something encouraging. "Sure, there's a lot of work right now, but once we build the *Mrs Crane* like Dad says, we'll all work together and it'll be fun. Dad says the fun never stops on a fishing boat."

"Dad says a lot of things."

"Yeah. I know." September saw that Ivan was calming down and moved closer.

Ivan picked up his clam bucket and rake. "Sep, do you really think we'll build the *Mrs Crane* this year?"

"Dad says so."

"But what do *you* think?"

September cast around for something to say and noticed the *Aunt Nelda* high and dry and the clams squirting around her like a comical park fountain. "I think we better get to these clams while we can. We've got two radios to pay for."

September started back to the boat for her bucket and rake with Ivan right on her heels. "You didn't answer my question. Do you think we'll get the new boat?"

September kept moving. "I don't know, Ivan," she admitted. "I hope so."

"You sound like Dad again."

September pulled her gear out of the dinghy and turned to her brother. "I was trying to sound like me." She paused and pulled on the heavy work gloves that would let her scrounge around in the cold and jagged beach stones. "Listen, Ivan, I get mad sometimes too. I'm mad right now because I'm digging clams to pay for your stupid mistake so that we don't have to stay at Aunt Nelda's every time Dad leaves.

"This has nothing to do with Dad," she continued, indicating the clam bed at their feet oozing seawater and bright green algae. "And the rest of it? Well, I do know that Dad can't be here in Steamer Cove taking care of us and out there at Dutch Harbor making money for the *Mrs Crane* at the same time. He's got his job and we've got ours. We're a family. That's how it works."

"That's what he says, all right." Ivan turned away and dragged his hand rake through the mucky gravel at the water's edge. In the ripe-smelling mire of a minus tide he saw nearly a dozen steamer clams churn into view.

"Hooeey! Money in the bank!" he called exactly the way his father always did. He'd said it without thinking, and he had to smile for the first time all day.

September laughed and triumphantly ripped her own rake into the mess. It had taken some smooth talking, but seeing Ivan smile again was worth more than all the clams in Steamer Cove.

"Money in the bank!" she echoed, and the steady plunk of clams hitting empty buckets filled the beach.

Ivan could never get used to the smell of low tide on a warm day. It was like a combination of old milk, wet shoes, and the dead stuff dogs find to roll in all mixed together. The clams were well worth the stink, though.

Ivan guessed that it took twenty clams to make a pound. So at one dollar to a pound each clam was worth five cents. As he scratched away and chucked clam after clam into his bucket, he counted off by nickels and dollars to entertain himself. Ninety...ninety-five...one dollar! So by the time the tide had risen far enough to float the *Aunt Nelda* and drive them up the beach beyond where the beds were thickest, they knew exactly where they stood regarding the high finance of clams.

"Ten bucks in a bucket." Ivan dropped two last steamers on top of his full load. "Darn near exactly!"

September straddled her brimming pail while she fetched the dory back to shore with the bowline. "This only took us a couple of hours. We'll have our sixty bucks' worth by Thursday, no problem."

"Can we get everything else done, too?"

September pitched the coiled line into the bow of the *Aunt Nelda* and stepped in after it, awkwardly heaving the bucket of clams along with her. "We better."

Ivan handed over his bucket. "But what if we don't?"

"If we don't, then we're going to have some explaining to do when Dad gets home. And if we explain anything, we'll have to explain *everything*."

"Not the radios!" Ivan begged.

"Radios, town, everything," September said firmly. "Dad knows we can get all this work done because we always do. If we don't, he'll know something's wrong. So let's not mess this up by feeling sorry for ourselves anymore. We're going to work harder than ever. Deal?"

Ivan shoved the boat clear of the beach and hopped in. "Deal."

"Good," she said, moving to the seat in the stern and pointing at the middle one. "It's your turn to row."

◆ ◆ ◆

At the sound of a rifle shot, everything with ears in Steamer Cove jumped. A long afternoon of work came to a sudden halt. The family of ravens living in the rock cliffs opposite Berger's place sprang from their nests and thrashed at the air, squawking in great disapproval. The loons blooped underwater and submarined to some hidden nook. A squirrel on the roof of the outhouse, which had been coaching Ivan's steady progress digging the new latrine, went still as taxidermy. September froze in midstride with a crate of deep-purple jars of freshly canned beets. The end of Ivan's shovel was all that showed above the hole.

"What was that?" Ivan said.

September breathed again and cast a mean eye toward their neighbor. "Mooseburger shooting at something again." She shaded her eyes to the sun just setting in the clear sky behind the ridge but could not see him or any sign of what the old man might be firing at.

"He better not have shot our little bear." Ivan, covered in black peat, crabbed up and over the edge of the pit and squatted, holding his shovel as if he would beat somebody on the head with it. The black bear, no bigger than a large dog, paid regular visits to the cove and was interested in little more than the berries and the warm late day hillsides—perfect for napping. He'd even walked right past the smokehouse one day, stopped for a sniff, then loped on into the underbrush again. A good bear to have for a neighbor, thought Ivan. Unlike some neighbors. "That old freak."

"Don't worry. He never hits anything he shoots at. Dad says as poorly as ol' Mooseburger sees without his telescope, he shouldn't even be handling a gun."

September set her crate down. "Besides, I saw our little blackie cleaning up the last of those blueberries over on the south ridge just a while ago. He'll be eating his way down to the marsh in Huckleberry Cove for the devil's club berries by now."

Ivan pointed his shovel at Berger's cabin. "Why do you think he shoots his guns like that?"

"Dad says it's because he's scared and lonely and wants the world to know he's here. So once a week or so he has to make some noise."

Ivan spit the dirt from around his mouth. "I think he does it to let us know he's watching."

"Same thing."

September leaned over the hole in the ground. "Looks good."

Ivan brushed himself off. "Good enough for what it's for."

The sun dropped out of sight and a sudden coolness filled the cove. It passed through Ivan and September, who felt it right to the quick now that they'd stopped working.

"Let's call it a day and get some supper." September shook off the chill and walked her crate of beets up to the porch.

Ivan was afraid to ask but did anyway. "What's for dinner?"

"Salmon patties and beets."

"Beets taste like dirt," he muttered.

September looked back at her blackened sibling. "Anything would taste like dirt in your condition. I tell you what—you take a sponge bath over at the sauna so I can be sure you're my brother, and I'll break out the last can of spaghetti and meatballs from town."

"Yesss!" Ivan speared his shovel into the loose dirt next to the privy. Peeling his shirt over his head, he stumbled straight into the hole he'd spent all afternoon digging.

September stared at the empty place where her brother had just been. "Ivan?"

"Don't say a word," the hole said.

September let the porch door bang closed behind her and lit a lamp in the dim interior. It felt good to have Ivan back to normal again.

CHAPTER 6

"How come everything from town tastes better?" Ivan slurped up the last stray spaghetti noodle.

"Does it?" September looked up sleepily from her clean plate.

"Sure. You name any food we get over here, and I'll tell you one from town that's better."

"Moose steaks," September said.

"Cheeseburgers."

"I'll give you that one. Baked potatoes."

"French fries."

"Okay, I'll give you that too." September had a sly smile on her face. "I've got one for you."

"Go for it."

"Fresh blueberries with fireweed honey."

"That's two things," Ivan said.

"Not if Dad's gone," September said mischievously.

"Okay, then…" Ivan tapped at his lips. "Chocolate shakes!" He didn't sound convinced.

"Be honest, Ivan. You know how you are about berries and honey."

"Call that a tie then. What else?" he challenged.

September looked like a poker player with an ace up her sleeve. "Smoked king salmon."

"No fair. There's *nothing* like smoked king salmon," Ivan admitted.

"And there's nothing like French fries." September ended the debate with a truce. "There are good things on both sides of the bay."

Ivan stood to gather up the plates and yawned long and loud. "I'm just glad my bed is on this side of the bay tonight."

"You said it." September fell onto her bed alongside the stove and gathered up the school papers she'd started reading. It took everything she had to keep her eyes open while Ivan did the dishes.

"Clam tide first thing in the morning," she reminded him.

"Money in the bank," Ivan answered eventually, but by then he was already talking to himself.

The clinking of dishes came into September's dream as gold coins dropping into clam buckets then turning into showers of coins. Ol' Mooseburger walked down the beach toward them through a thick fog with a rifle in his hands and the little black bear by his side. Berger raised the rifle and a shot lifted September right out of her bed.

Ivan stood inside the door, a dripping shadow in the gray morning light. "It's raining out, Sep."

Ivan dropped her rain gear on the kitchen chair. "And it's time to dig clams again."

◆ ◆ ◆

55

It *was* raining out. The rain of that day ran into the next and all of the next and well into the one after that. A straight-down flat-out rain that hissed at their every effort and began to wash the world of its lovely September color. The orange bursts of birch leaves and yellow blasts of alder became patches of pale bone-colored smears through the darkening woods. The bright green low growth of huckleberry bush and fern went brown like old lettuce. The scarlet crowns of berries atop the thorny devil's club were all that stood proud. The last of the overripe blueberries fell into rivulets of rain and were pounded to pulp on their tumble through the weeds and stones leading to the sea.

Ivan ducked back under the porch roof where September presided over the can cooker. "Are we the only living things dumb enough to be out in this?" He'd just finished bailing the rainwater from the boats and checking on their sixty dollars' worth of bagged clams. He looked back out across their drenched domain. The rain had slowed them down some, but they'd worked steadily through it.

They could barely make out a narrow line of smoke snaking from Berger's chimney, the only sign of him they'd seen in three days. Ivan watched two sea otters back-paddle in at high tide to dive for clams and an unlucky crab or two. They looked perfectly content in the downpour. It figures, thought Ivan, of an animal that spends its entire life afloat.

"I'm going to grow webbed feet if this keeps up," he complained.

"We're almost finished here." September loosened the lid on the pressure cooker and spoke through the cloud of steam. "This is the last batch. Once these cool, we'll be done with the canning for now. Dad might want to put up some more zucchini, but we should wait to see how many he wants to pickle first."

"So that's it then." Ivan wrung the water out of his work gloves and wiped his hands on their dad's old coverall, which hung by a nail from the porch post next to the generator bike. "And tomorrow's town day."

"Weather permitting," September cautioned. "Without a radio to tell us what's coming, we're not leaving this cove in anything but a dead calm."

"Rain or shine?" Ivan looked hopefully at his sister.

"Rain or shine doesn't matter," she said importantly, relishing Ivan's worry. "But if it blows, then it's no go."

"Big blow a no go," Ivan teased.

September laughed. "But if it *doesn't* blow, then it's a go-go."

"No blow a go-go. Check." Ivan mock-saluted the instructions.

Their good spirits could not be dampened by the nagging rain. They had worked like wheel dogs for the last four days—heads down the whole way. And they'd accomplished all of the week's chores except for the new coat of paint on the *Aunt Nelda*. A boat can't be painted in the rain and their dad would understand. They'd managed to get the outhouse skidded across the mud to the new hole, which would surely impress their father. They had all next week to fill the wood boxes and drain the water line from the spring box for winter. And since they wouldn't have to spend every morning sniffing the muck across the cove for clams, they might be able to stay awake long enough at night to tackle their schoolwork.

"You think we got enough clams?" September wondered.

"Yeah, I think so. But we better go again in the morning. We need to get some more butter clams for Dad's stews. I haven't been finding too many."

"No, me either." September looked out through the porch roof dribble. "I know a better spot up closer to Mooseburger's end. We'll go check there before we head to town. The best clam tides are all done for the month, and we'd have a hard time explaining why we didn't get his butters."

Ivan tipped the water from the cooker onto the ground. "And we'd hear about it every time he thought of clam chowder."

"Twice a day," September agreed, starting through the door. "After you wash that out, why don't you fire up the sauna so we can get cleaned up for town."

Ivan looked slyly over his shoulder. "Watch out, TC. She's washing her hair!"

"You have an overactive imagination, Ivan Crane." September spoke calmly but couldn't get her red cheeks inside the cabin quite in time to hide them from her brother.

"A go-go and a goo-goo too." Ivan hooted at his own wit all the way out to the sauna.

The rain drilled steadily at the cabin roof. September dried her hair with a brush and towel next to the stove. Ivan took the teapot from on top and poured hot water into two mugs.

"Mmm," September said, closing her eyes. "I love the smell of rose-hip tea."

"Dad says Mom gave us this when we got wet hair." Ivan handed September her tea, and she nodded.

"Mom said it was good for colds. The smell always reminds me of her."

The steam rose out of the mug and fell back in on itself. September blew it clear and took a sip. Ivan sat facing the window, holding his mug between his raised knees. Rain tracked down the black windowpanes, reflecting like shooting stars in the lamplight.

"Do you remember, Sep?"

"Remember what?" She knew what, and blinked at the rain trails on the window.

"The night Mom died." Ivan pulled his knees up closer.

"Sort of."

"Tell me."

Ivan stayed facing the rainy glass. September looked for the memory. So little to tell. But Ivan had never asked before. So long now. So far. So...

"One of us had a fever. Maybe both, I don't remember. Dad put us to bed—back there—in their bed. You were asleep but I was listening to the storm. I could hear trees breaking clear up the hill. Dad kept going outside to look at things. The wind rattled the chimney and when it really roared the lamp on the table would flicker." September sipped her tea and looked around the room. She noticed the loose wires behind the kitchen table.

"I could hear Dad talking on the radio. *Turn back*, he'd say. *You have to go back*, he said. But I couldn't hear anyone talking to him. Only static sounding just like the wind. Then there was a noise outside like those jets in Anchorage. Like they were coming right up on the porch. The whole house shook. The light fluttered out and I called 'Daddy' and he came in to be with us. 'Williwaw, Temmy,' he told me, and held on to us both. It growled like a bear right under the bed for the longest time and I could hear pieces of the woods hitting the wall and pieces of the cabin coming off and you started crying and I started crying and Dad just held on to us. 'Williwaw,' he said again when it quit, and he went back out to the radio."

Ivan was looking at his sister now, the tea forgotten in his hands. "When did you know?"

"Men came the next day. Harry and others, I don't remember who. All I really remember about that day is the orca in the cove."

"A killer whale in the cove?" Ivan had never heard of this.

"No—orca. Dad says never call them killers. But yes, there was an orca swimming around the cove. I was so excited about it. I wanted to be on the dock to get close, and Dad walked me to the end. I remember laughing and clapping my hands every time it blew. Dad and the men let me have my fun, and eventually the whale left. No one had ever seen that before, and no one's seen it since." September looked at the question remaining in her brother's eyes.

"I don't remember when he told me." September patted the towel to her face once and tried a smile. "I've lost that. The whale is what I remember most."

They sipped at their tea and listened to the rain pass. The fire shifted in the stove and flared. The ruffle of the flame was the loudest thing in the room until a loon called its lonesome night song through the calm. Ivan spoke next.

"I was reading in my geography lesson the other night how in

India they believe people can come back as all kinds of animals, and cows can lay right down in the road there and nobody even bothers them." Ivan looked again at his sister. "Do you think people can come back as animals, Sep?"

"Sure. Why not?"

"You ever think Mom came back as one?"

September knew where the conversation was heading. "Maybe."

"Which one?"

Ivan sounded eager, even impatient, but September took time with this idea.

"All of them," she said. "At different times I think maybe she's all of them."

"How?" Ivan urged.

"I don't know *how*, Ivan. This isn't a science project. All I know is that sometimes when I'm walking in the woods a squirrel will pop up and chatter at me and I'll look at it and think *Mom?* Or I'll see a cow moose walking with two calves in the summertime and she'll raise her head and look at me for the longest time, as if she knows me."

Ivan was intrigued. "How about the little bear?"

"Sure. Comes around to visit all the time. Doesn't bother anything. You think Mom would come back and raid the smoker?"

Ivan laughed and tried to think of others. There were plenty to consider, and as he did he realized all of them had at least some small share of the qualities a mom might have. Eagles watching overhead and hauling food to the nest. Wolves walking softly and singing to the moon. Skilled beavers building impossibly clever homes and dams from a self-logged forest. And there was another.

"How about orcas, Sep? Do you think she's that too?"

September folded her towel across her lap and grew still. "Could be," she said not much louder than the rain. "At least one time I thought so."

Ivan looked into his empty cup and said nothing. September set hers on the table and turned the lamp down. She put a hand on Ivan's shoulder. "You okay?"

"Yeah," he said. "Thanks for that. I never knew what really happened."

"Dad didn't tell me the whole story. I still don't know what happened out on the bay that night. Maybe someday he'll tell us both about it." September put the lamp out and found her bed. "When he's ready."

"Maybe so." Ivan crawled under his blankets and felt sleep coming over him. "Good night, Sep."

"Good night, Ivan."

A loon cried in the cove. Another, sounding far away, answered in the same plaintive tone.

"Good night, Mom," they said, and slept.

CHAPTER 7

The morning fog was dense. So dense it felt almost heavy on Ivan's and September's heads as they made their careful way across the cove in the *Aunt Nelda*. Their world was cloaked so completely they hadn't been able to see the cabin from their own dock, and they'd lost sight of that too as soon as they'd shoved off. The stillness bordered on deadness—black water as shiny as a waxed table and no sound but the dull rattle of the oarlocks.

They knew Mooseburger's cabin was due west of theirs and the butter clam bed a little south of that. September sat in the stern holding a hand compass between them so that Ivan could watch their bearing as he rowed the short way over.

"I've never seen it this thick," he said, staring into a mist so formless that his eyes could find no focus.

September blinked away the same effect. "Me either. Everything seems so different—like we're not even real." She checked their heading again and was about to suggest a correction when the dory nudged quietly onto a soft bottom and swung to a stop.

"Weird," she said, and stepped over the side into a few inches of water. Paying careful attention to the depth of the water as she circled the boat, September came to the conclusion that they were not on a bar but on Mooseburger's mud flat—exactly where they wanted to be. "Let's go find Dad's butter clams."

Ivan climbed out with a bucket. He uncoiled the bowline and then followed September slowly into the murk. After only a few steps they found dry ground and the welcome sight of clams spitting all around their feet. "Good navigating," Ivan said.

"Hard to get lost in Steamer Cove." September smiled and leaned into the familiar smells and motions.

The scrape of their rakes and the clatter of clams hitting the empty bucket seemed a grating intrusion in the quiet mist. September felt self-conscious about it, knowing Mr. Berger was not far off. "Did you hear something, Ivan?" she asked.

Ivan stopped and listened. "No—wait—could it be? Yes…the sound of a video game. A video game in my future…" A grin stretched his face, and he cupped a hand around one ear. "Hello? Tech Patrol?"

September wasn't amused. "Ivan, you have got a one-track mind. It was your game addiction that started all this trouble. Now we can't even see the boat on the end of the line in your hand and you're ready to head across the bay for another video fix."

Ivan looked panicked. "Sep! You promised if it wasn't blowing we'd go. It's flat as a board out there. We've gone all the way to town by compass before!"

September held up her hands. "Okay, okay! Stop whining. We'll go. We have to. But remember, we're going to get the radios first of all. We'll go to the Dockside only if we have the money, the time, and the coast is clear. Deal?"

"Deal," Ivan said, relieved.

September looked back into the fog. "It would be nice if this lifted a little."

Suddenly she seized on movement in the near distance. She worked her eyes around in their sockets, not sure if it was just a trick of the fog. But it still moved, slowly and deliberately, toward them. "Ivan, look!"

Ivan turned, and they both stood rock-still. They could hear the grind of boots in gravel and then the sucking sounds of the mud grabbing at footsteps. A dark blot turned suddenly human as it came out of the mist not ten steps away. Mr. Berger, his black wool coat with the hood pulled around his face against the damp chill, stood wide-legged in his hip boots with a rifle cradled across his chest.

September went nearly faint with this picture out of her dream standing so close at hand. She even glanced around to see if the little bear was along before she refocused on the old man with the gun. He was no dream.

"Mr. Berger!" September blustered. "You scared us!"

"So it's you two!" Berger stood firm in the mud. "You're lucky I didn't shoot you! What are you wild coyotes up to sneaking around my property?" he asked.

The scowling old man cast a hard look at the partially filled bucket. "So that's it! Stealing clams under the cover of the fog!" he accused them.

"We didn't mean to!" Ivan said, forgetting in his fear that nobody owns the tide flats and the clams belong to everybody. "We just wanted to get some butter clams to can for our dad before he gets home."

September tried to nudge her brother, but it was too late. Berger screwed his head to one side and looked back at them with new suspicion. "I've been wondering if that father of yours was ever coming back." A satisfied grin revealed a mouthful of brown mottled teeth. "I've been wondering if I ought to go talk to somebody in town about the situation out here."

"No!" September blurted more loudly than she'd meant to. "I mean, there's no need. We're fine, and besides, our dad is coming home today." She knocked Ivan with her knee. "We're going to pick him up as soon as we're done with these clams—right, Ivan?"

Ivan's face quizzed his sister and she drilled him with a look. "Umm—that's right, Mr. Berger. Dad's coming in from Dutch Harbor on the two-thirty plane." Ivan glanced around. "I guess we better get moving if we're going to make it in time."

September grabbed up the bucket. "That's right. It'll be slow going in this stuff." She started backing away, and after giving a little tug to Ivan's jacket, her brother followed.

Mr. Berger screwed his head over even farther and looked as mean as a mink in a live trap. "I'll tell you wild brats one thing! If that so-called father of yours ain't back here today to keep you out of my hair, I'm going to the authorities!" He raised the rifle and laid it back over his shoulder as September and Ivan receded into the mist. "You hear me. Flame-baked hooligans! The authorities!"

"Yes, sir. He'll be here!" September walked backward right into the *Aunt Nelda* and fell over into the bottom. "Push off, Ivan!" she commanded before she even got herself upright.

"I'm pushing! I'm pushing!"

As soon as the dory floated free of the mud, September was on the oars digging at the water. Ivan grabbed the compass. The instrument's needle stabilized. "That way, Sep!" he said, and pointed. "That's the way back!"

They made the distance home in less time than it took them to sort through all the implications of their meeting with Berger. As the *Aunt Nelda* knocked against their dock, Ivan climbed out and tied the dory off.

"Why'd you tell him Dad was coming home today, Sep?"

September stepped onto the dock, her heart still pounding from the experience. "I had to! You heard what he said!"

Ivan started up the dock squinting into the mist toward the cabin. "I know, and if Mooseburger calls the state people while Dad's gone, they'll have no choice but to take us away," he said. "But what's going to happen when he finds out Dad *isn't* coming home today and we lied?"

September stopped short as she looked at the porch. She seized Ivan by the hand. "Ivan, what's that?"

Ivan looked ahead and saw it too—something, or *someone*, was standing against one of the support posts. Then his eyes saw through the illusion of fog.

"Oh, that's just Dad's old coverall hanging up there. I guess Berger's got us both spooked." Ivan continued walking.

"I'll say." September followed her brother onto the porch and fingered the sleeve of the coverall as if to make sure it was empty. "And he's going to get us in big trouble when Dad doesn't show up today. Maybe I shouldn't have said that to Mr. Berger."

"Wait a minute," Ivan said, leaning against the railing. "What if Dad does show up?"

"And what if fish could walk?" September quipped.

"I don't mean *really* show up. Just if ol' Mooseburger *thought* he did?"

Intrigued, September let go of the coverall and sat down beside Ivan. "What are you thinking?"

Before he spoke, Ivan studied the cobwebs in the rafters above his head as if that's where his thoughts were. "How would Berger know if Dad is with us or not when we come back from town today?"

"He'll either be with us or he won't," September said impatiently.

"Will Berger come over and talk to him?" he quizzed.

"Of course not. He never does."

"Then how will he know?"

September grew exasperated. "He'll *see* him! I mean, he *won't* see him!"

"That's *exactly* right!" Ivan said with a cagey grin. "He'll see him and he won't see him. Ol' Mooseburger can't see much better than we can see right now in this fog. So what if we made something that *looked* like Dad and brought it home in the boat with us today?"

He slid from the railing, grabbed the worn coverall from its hook, and held it up as if modeling a dress. "If you thought this was someone standing on the porch, what do you think this would look like to a half-blind old Mooseburger?"

September now grasped what Ivan was thinking. She cocked

one eye at the dirty work suit being dragged along the porch like a starved scarecrow. "One coverall doesn't make a dad. What will fill it out? And what about a head?" she asked skeptically.

"Details. Simply details." Ivan dramatically laid the thing over the seat of the generator bike and considered it. "All we gotta do is stuff it full of something…"

"We could use leaves, no, I know—sawdust! We could fill it with sawdust and wood chips from the mill." September cried. "We go right past it in town. We'll go over where it spills out by the loading dock and fill it!"

"Perfect!" Ivan said, happy to see his serious-minded sister getting into the swing of it. "And for a head we can cram one of those smaller crab-pot buoys down the neck hole and tie a nor'easter over that." Ivan took one of the floppy heavy weather rain hats from their pile of boat gear and held it over the coverall.

September eyed the effect suspiciously. "How long do you think this will keep Mr. Berger off our backs?"

"Long enough," Ivan said, and then peered into the fog. "Or at least as long as ol' Mooseburger stays on his side of the cove."

The week's clam harvest had been kept alive in burlap bags hanging from the end of the dock. While Ivan gathered them together, September ran to the cabin and grabbed herself a snack of smoked salmon on dried bread. She scarfed it, then quickly made another to take to Ivan.

"Something for the ride," she said, handing over the sandwich and looking out to the bay. "This fog hasn't thinned one bit. It's going to take forever to get to town—over an hour, probably." Ivan munched and watched his sister check the fuel line to the motor. "How's our gas situation?"

September hefted the can currently in use. "We'll get there on what's left of this can. Three times across, as always. The other can is full but we *have* to get fuel today and replace what we've used."

"We'll have plenty of money." Ivan wiped his hands on his pants, then lowered the last of the clams into the *Four-O-Five*. "We'll have money for a lot of things."

Ivan had a familiar look in his eye and September shook her head. "Ivan, you are going to get video-game poisoning one day."

"What a way to go," he said, smiling.

Ivan decided not to argue over who steered the skiff. Since it would be such a monotonous ride in the fog anyway, he'd rather wait his turn for the way back when it all might be cleared. Looking straight up he could almost see blue sky.

September strained to see what she could as she steered the *Four-O-Five* out of the cove. It wouldn't take long for the fog to burn off or blow away, but in the meantime she couldn't see thirty feet. Luckily the tide was flooding hard and left patterns in the water where the rocks lay. Once clear of the point she took their regular compass heading, checked the time, and sped up to about half throttle. With the bay so calm it was tempting to go faster, but without being able to see what might be in the water ahead she remained, as ever, on the better side of caution. "Bag Bay loves overconfident skippers," Dad had said a thousand times. "It eats them for lunch."

"Keep your eyes out for logs, Ivan!" she said.

In an hour's time the only change in the monotony of fog and flat water was a swath of gunk caught in a tide rip, which September slowed to pass through. She knew the oozy-looking collection of sticks, loose kelp, and trash could be hiding submerged logs that would do considerable damage to a boat and motor if hit at any speed.

When they were past the danger, September resumed her previous course and speed. She looked again at the compass. Thirty-three degrees north northeast for one hour. She looked at her wristwatch. We should be close, she thought.

September also found herself thinking that the town kids would still be in school at this hour on a Thursday, and this gave her a surprising stab of disappointment. Although she would never admit it to her brother, she had been looking forward to this strange TC kid being nice to her right out in front of the townie girls again. She'd already recalled the scene a dozen times.

September smiled at the memory but swallowed it away when she saw Ivan impatiently looking at her from the bow. He pointed at his wrist for the time, and it was with horror September saw that twenty more minutes had passed on her watch with no town in sight. She slowed the motor to an idle and dropped it out of gear. The two of them and their boatful of clams bobbed as the wake of the *Four-O-Five* overtook them.

"Uh-oh." Ivan stood up and looked hard into the vapor surrounding them.

September checked the compass and pointed. "That's where we should have seen it by now."

"Are you sure you stayed on course?" Ivan wasn't accusing. He'd steered in the fog enough times to know that as soon as you looked away from the compass even the most seasoned boat handler could veer off-course.

September flushed and admitted, "I wasn't paying attention for a while there. I might have drifted."

"Which way?" Ivan couldn't keep the concern out of his voice. Missing the harbor to the east would bring them harmlessly down that shore by the sawmill, which they could follow back to the harbor. But missing to the west meant bypassing the point and heading straight out into the open waters leading to the Gulf of Alaska.

Both of them knew the best thing they could possibly do was nothing. Guessing would be the worst. They could be a hundred feet from the beach on the other side of town, or in a six-hundred-foot-deep subarctic sea with roaming cargo ships and oil tankers. Until they knew on which side of the point they were, the compass was nearly useless—only good for taking a bearing once they saw or heard something that they could follow to safety. Neither of them said a word. Their best chance was to hear a honking car horn or the clank of heavy machinery at the mill, and they would have to stay silent to catch it. Another boat might happen by on its way to who knows where, but unless they could get its attention, it would be no use to them. September opened the toolbox and put the signal-flare pistol on the seat beside her. Ivan relaxed a little. Although neither would say it, both of them feared being run down by a larger boat or a tanker out in the big water. It would have been easier to hear without the idling motor, but they couldn't take the chance of being dead in the water and unable to dodge an approaching vessel.

Ivan suddenly pointed to something off their right side—coming straight toward them. With nothing to reference the dark shape against, it could be a deep-sea trawler a quarter mile away or a large duck within a clam's throw.

"An otter." September finally breathed. "It's just an otter with her young one."

Ivan could see it now too. A sea otter paddled along on her back with her arms wrapped around her baby. As soon as September spoke, the otter started a slow curve out of the way. She and her little one swam from view leaving a tiny V-shaped wake and never taking their eyes from the odd pair of creatures in the skiff.

No sooner had the otter gone than a black and white torpedo at least the size of the *Four-O-Five* burst into view with a rush of wind.

"Orca!" Ivan screamed. September jumped.

The long curved dorsal fin cut beneath the looking-glass bay and...

Nothing.

Orcas often took several breaths before diving again so they waited to hear another blow from the whale. But none ever came.

The ripples from the whale's grand appearance made chuckling sounds against the bottom of the skiff. Ivan felt the boat swinging around, then sensed movement across his face.

"A breeze, Sep. Look!" The mist was clearly in motion, scudding soundlessly across the water. The lightweight skiff began to move with it. The breeze would be sure to push the fog out but was of no immediate help.

"It's from the east," September said, brightening as she looked up from the compass. An east wind was most likely coming off the glacier in the mountains behind town, which meant they were probably still inside the bay. But then again, maybe not. If they were already beyond the point and headed east, they wouldn't find shore until the steep cliffs of Rocky Point way up by Port Vixen. They would certainly run out of gas in both tanks before then.

Ivan read her mind. "Wanna guess and go?"

"No way." September pulled her hat down over her ears. "Dad says guesses make messes."

Ivan silently agreed and kept his face to the breeze. Come on, give me something—anything, he thought. He sniffed at the air and his nostrils flared. *What? Could it be?* He took a long, deep pull…."Yesss!" He pointed into the wind, laughing. "Town ahoy!"

September tried to see. "Where? Where?"

"Don't look! Smell! I can smell it!" Ivan threw his head back and breathed in with exaggerated delight.

September looked doubtful but followed her brother's lead and sniffed generally around in the air. Sure enough, there was something. *What was that smell?*

"French fries!" Ivan spoke before she could place it. "Greasy Dockside French fries dead ahead!"

It was good enough to go on. September pointed the skiff

into the breeze and took a compass heading while Ivan leaned over the bow sniffing like a dog out a car window and singing.

"*East wind blows you side to side and sometimes even smells like fries!*"

They had gone only a few hundred feet this way when the motor sputtered. Ivan hushed. September shook the gas can at her feet.

"Empty!" she called, working the throttle back and forth to milk what fuel she could from the line.

Ivan jumped to the back of the boat and tried to change the cans before the motor quit, but it was too late. The outboard coughed twice, rattled once, then fell silent as they coasted into the fog.

Clipping the gas line to the new tank, Ivan apologized. "Sorry, Sep. Missed it."

CHAPTER 8

"My fault," September said, squeezing the primer bulb. "I should have checked while we were idling. I guess we cut it too close on that tank."

She stood and grabbed the starter cord. Ivan held the throttle and choke while September yanked the cord time after time.

"Your turn," she gasped, trading places with Ivan.

"I hate it when we let this run completely dry. It's so hard to get started again." Ivan took his share of fruitless pulls, then September tried again.

"Good thing it's so calm. Can you imagine doing this in rough water?"

"No way," he said woefully.

September took a determined grip and threw her whole body with the pull. Ivan nursed the throttle. The motor sneezed like a horse three times. "C'mon, baby," Ivan encouraged, teasing the throttle like rolling dice. The sneeze became a belch of blue smoke, and the motor warbled to life and revved clean. "Go-go-go!" Ivan cheered.

September shook some life into her spent arm and took the tiller again. I'll be very happy when this star-crossed week is over, she thought as she steered them carefully into the French-fry-flavored air.

As it happened, they had been a few hundred yards from the harbor entrance, and it took just minutes to sweep around the end of the sea wall into the vague but familiar gangs of boats at dock. Even now the fog was so thick that they could see neither shape nor sign of any town beyond the lazy port.

"I guess we don't have to worry about Harry catching us this trip," September said as she nudged the *Four-O-Five* up behind the harbor master's shack.

"Or anybody else for that matter." Ivan shed his boat gear and hefted a drooping sack of clams in each hand. "We better get these up to the fish company while they're still worth something."

September grabbed two of her own and swung them onto the dock. "I don't think it could have taken us any longer to get here if we'd rowed over."

"Don't even say it, Sep. We've had enough bad luck for one day."

September continued unloading their catch. "Bad luck is being lost at sea with an oil tanker plowing you under. I'd say smelling Dockside fries out of nowhere is pretty good luck by comparison."

"Good old Dockside." Ivan grinned, and they both started working a little bit faster.

◆ ◆ ◆

"Eighty dollars!" Ivan slammed the door to the fish buyer's office and leaped into the air. "We got eighty dollars, Sep!"

September breathed easier seeing the splay of twenty-dollar bills Ivan fanned in front of her. They'd be able to pay for the radios, and this whole sorry ordeal would be finished. Then she looked cautiously over his shoulder at the office door. "Did they ask any questions?"

Ivan shrugged. "They just asked where Dad was, and I said he had other things to do."

September's mouth tightened. "I don't like all this sneaking around and lying. Every time we tell a lie we get in this deeper."

"It wasn't a lie! He *is* doing other things. It's not my fault he's doing them in the Bering Sea."

"I still don't like it. Dad's never going to trust us again if he finds out."

Ivan flagged the money in her face as he started away. "Lighten up, Sep. Dad's not going to find out. C'mon, let's go have some fun!"

"Not so fast, Little Mister." September reached out and snagged a twenty before Ivan could pull it away. "You get those radios and I'm going to go find those fries we've been smelling."

"Save some for me!" Ivan said, already trotting around the corner and out of sight.

"No way," September said softly, making her way along the boardwalk to the Dockside.

◆ ◆ ◆

The bells on the Dockside door tinkled when she entered. The only person September saw was the rumpled woman behind the counter, who barely looked up from her paperback book.

"Good afternoon," September said.

"I suppose it is," the woman mumbled.

"Could I have some French fries and a chocolate milkshake? Please?"

"Hnn," the woman grunted, but made no move to do so. September fidgeted at the counter, not sure whether to sit down or offer money. She was relieved when the door bells jangled behind her. Expecting her brother, she spoke before she'd turned completely around.

"You want fries and a shake too?" She cast her eyes to the figure in the doorway and then stood blank-eyed as a seagull in a tide rip.

"Don't mind if I do!" TC replied, and walked straight toward her.

"Oh!" September found her voice. "I thought you were Ivan."

TC leaned against the counter in a big, loose way. "Is that your brother? The kid I saw last week?"

"Yeah. We just came over to sell some clams and pick up our radios." September didn't know why she would tell this information to an almost perfect stranger. She flushed with regret that she'd given up the secret so easily.

TC didn't seem to care. He looked out the window into the thick ground fog moving lazily up the street. "You guys came across the bay in this weather? How?"

September laughed, partly from nerves but mostly at TC's curiosity over the most ordinary things. You would think they'd just climbed down from a moon rocket. "We use a compass when it's like this. It's not that hard."

The woman behind the counter was finally moving and TC said, "I'll have what she's having."

"Hmmff," the woman said, and TC walked across the snack bar indicating a table to September.

"Weren't you afraid of getting lost?"

September sat down. "Actually, we did, but then we smelled the French fries at this place and came right to it."

TC wagged his head in amazement. "You sniffed your way here. Awesome!"

September smiled warily, not sure what to make of TC's enthusiasm. No one in town had ever showed the slightest interest in her before. She gave TC's gearhead bike jacket the once-over. "Where are you from? Not from around here, I'd guess."

"Seattle. Me and my mom just moved here."

"Where's your dad?" she asked, just to make conversation.

"Divorced." TC's voice dropped a little on the word. "How about you?"

September knew what he meant but couldn't resist saying, "I've never even been married."

They laughed together easily, then TC asked again. "I mean your parents. Where are they?"

"Our mom died, and Dad is...um"—she had a harder time with the second part of the question than the first—"Dad's fishing."

TC again looked outside. "In this fog? When will he be back?"

September wasn't sure what to say at first. She squirmed in her chair while she searched her head for a good story, but all she came up with was truth. She wished Ivan were there. He was so much better at this. But, she thought, why lie to this kid? He was a little goofy, but no threat to them or their plan. He wouldn't know Harry or Aunt Nelda if they walked up and bit him. Finally, taking a sidelong look at the woman at the counter dishing their fries, September lowered her voice. "He'll be back next weekend. He's been gone two weeks."

TC almost came out of his chair. "You're alone over there?"

"Shhh!" September put her hand over TC's mouth, and that's just the pose the townie girls found them in when they came through the door.

The girls stood fidgeting under the tinkling bells.

"Hello, TC," one said flatly, then added, "I got the invitation to your party. Thanks, I'd love to come."

"Hi, Sheri. No problem." TC's friendly face did not change a fraction. "Sheri, Annette, do you know September?"

"You live across the bay, right?" Sheri said, coming to the table.

TC looked at September. "She and her brother came over in the fog today—with a compass!" he said with amazement.

The girls looked over September's plain brown wool coat and heavy canvas pants without expression. September's legs bumped nervously under the table. The rubber boots felt like tugboats on her feet. Annette was struggling for something to say, and September feared it wouldn't be very complimentary, so she was happy when the shakes and fries arrived to break the tension.

TC regarded the mass of French fries being laid out on the table. Without hesitation he invited Sheri and Annette to join them. Riveting his attention on September again, he said, "So how big is your boat? Is it fast? How far is your cabin?"

September picked out a French fry and gave it all her attention to avoid looking at the two edgy girls as they sat down.

"Why do you care so much about all that stuff?" she asked.

Sheri answered for TC. "He's a city boy. Don't you know? Been here two weeks and he still thinks Alaska is one big adventure park!"

She laughed as if anything could be so absurd, and with this September had to agree.

"It isn't all *that* exciting," she said, and pushed a plate of fries across to Sheri. "At least on our side of the bay."

"Well," Annette allowed, taking a fry for herself, "we don't have to worry about getting lost in the fog on our way to the Dockside."

"I don't know if you would call that excitement or *misery*," September remarked, and glowed when the others giggled.

TC tried to talk around the fresh hot fry he'd jammed into his mouth. "What about bears? Do you have to watch out for bears?"

Sheri and Annette groaned and said to September as if to include her in some long-suffered state of affairs, "He's obsessed with bears and boats."

"It's all he talks about."

September warmed to the girls, and liked being included in the gentle teasing about TC's excitable nature. He didn't seem to mind, and September didn't mind answering his questions.

"We do have one sweet little bear who comes through the cove all the time. Bears aren't mean by nature, you know. Everybody just thinks that because they're always chewing people up in the movies."

Sheri and Annette quietly munched their fries—apparently as willing as TC to hear about the little bear that came to visit. September had a royal time telling stories of the young bear scratching his belly on logs, napping in the berries, and scraping around in the kelp beds. The bear's antics led her to tell of their other animal neighbors: the fledgling eagles learning to fly; the mischievous raven family taunting them from on high; the otters and their clobbering rocks.

Annette and Sheri listened and nodded and joined in with their own experiences.

"Oh, I just think those otters are so cute!"

"And doesn't your heart melt when a seal looks at you? So sad and quiet."

They were no strangers to wild animals just because they lived in a town, and while they didn't have the intimate daily contact that September did, they were way out ahead of a Seattle slicker like TC.

"Wow," TC was saying for the tenth time as September finished describing their morning encounter with old Mooseburger and his rifle. "Would he really shoot you?"

Before she could answer, Ivan slunk through the door pathetically. He took in the three strangers at his sister's table and urgently waved her over to the far side of the store.

"I'll be right back," September said, getting up and noticing for the first time the empty plates on the table. "Uh-oh. We ate all the fries. And from the look on my brother's face he could use some."

TC jumped to his feet. "I'll get more."

September hurried over to Ivan. "Why don't you sit down? We're having a great time. And what took you so long?"

"We're toast, Sep."

"What's happened?"

"Nothing. Nothing's happened. The new radio parts were supposed to come in on today's plane, but it didn't land because of the fog. I waited at the shop for half an hour. Then the airport called and said the flight turned around and headed back to Anchorage. We don't have radios."

"When will we?"

"Saturday." Ivan made it sound like a hundred years away. "*If* they get the parts tomorrow."

"Too late." September's frame bent under the weight of this development.

TC breezed up to them on his way back from the snack counter. "What's up?" he asked, grinning a grin that tried to make everything okay. But it wasn't okay, and anyone, even a new friend, could see it on Ivan's and September's slack faces.

"What happened?" TC asked, his smile changing to a look of concern.

What happened? Ivan looked at his sister.

September looked at the floor. *What happened?* How could she explain that they were, in fact, toast. There was only one way out of this.

They told him. The whole long messy story from beginning to sad end. Their Dad's Friday-night call. The dreaded Aunt Nelda. Jump-wiring the video game on the wrong side of the power converter, and blitzing the radios. Sneaking to town—*twice*. Digging clams. Mr. Berger and their scarecrow-dad plan. It looked as if they were actually going to get away with it all—and now this.

By the end TC had led them back to the table, where Ivan ate like a condemned man—the fries his last meal.

"Yow," was all TC could say. "When you Alaskans go for trouble, you go all the way."

"Yow," Annette and Sheri agreed.

TC leaned into the table. "So what's your dad going to do when he can't reach you on the radio tomorrow night?"

"He's going to panic and call Harry to come check on us," September said. "But we can't let it go that far."

Ivan stopped eating and waited to hear the words he knew were coming.

September continued in a calm voice and spoke directly to her brother, as if the other kids weren't even in the room. "The game's over, Ivan. We've got to go tell Harry what happened."

Ivan resumed chewing and staring off into space like a sorry cow. He knew exactly what telling Harry meant. It meant going across on the *Williwaw* for their things at the cabin tonight or in the morning. Then they'd come back with Harry and be driven out to Aunt Nelda's homestead. Harry would tell of the whole escapade when their dad tried to reach them the following evening on the radio.

September thought of her father's sad silence after he heard the news, then he'd say, "I'm so disappointed." Her mind hummed with dread and she dropped her head into her hands as if to contain it all.

Annette and Sheri fiddled with their fingertips. TC chewed his lip awhile, then said, "What about Mr. Moosemeat?"

September saw this issue as the only bright spot. "Well, I guess nosy ol' Mooseburger will be satisfied. He'll see us come for our things with Harry and figure Dad never showed and we're going to stay with Aunt Nelda and Uncle Spitz. Which is exactly what we'll be doing. He'll have nothing to complain to the authorities about."

"Aunt Nelda and Uncle Spitz." Ivan repeated the names like reading a tombstone.

September wadded up her napkin and lobbed it across the table. "Don't cry to me about it, Ivan. You got us into this mess, and I'm paying for your stupidity. It's over. Get used to it."

TC leaned between the simmering siblings. "Hey, look on the bright side. You'll be on our end of the bay this weekend, and that means you can come to my party on Saturday."

Ivan perked up. "Party?"

"My birthday party. Right here! My mom is renting the whole

game room from ten in the morning until two! I'm inviting everyone. You come, too."

"Forget it, Ivan," September ordered. "After all this, I doubt Aunt Nelda's going to allow any parties."

Ivan ignored his sister and gaped at TC. "Even the Tech Patrol game?"

"*Especially* the Tech Patrol game." TC narrowed one eye. "Don't tell me you bush rats know about Tech Patrol?"

Ivan puffed. "I have every single comic book including the Invasion of the Four-Eyed Vipers series."

"Reading a comic book and sniping aliens on-screen are two different things." TC rose from his chair and drew his fingers like pistols. "Care to challenge the master?"

Ivan gooned a pleading face to his sister who had already crossed her eyes over the boys' video jabber. "Puh-*leeez*, Sep! Do we have time?"

"You are definitely hopeless," September said sadly, and then checked her watch. Seeing it was still the middle of the afternoon, she shrugged. "Why not? I suppose we have to do something until Harry gets back. Thursdays he has his Port Vixen run, and he doesn't usually get back until after six. Enjoy it while you still can."

"All right!" With a jingle of quarters Ivan and TC vanished into the adjoining arcade.

September watched them go and heaved a great sigh. "He's going to die from those video games someday."

Sheri smirked. "Boys are boys. No matter where they come from."

"Sad but true."

87

They all burst out laughing, and then Annette blurted, "For a bush rat you seem pretty normal."

The three grew silent for a long moment. The whiz-bang of laser cannons and photon explosions edged in from next door. September glanced outside and saw the bay was blown nearly clear of fog. She felt a long way from home, yet oddly grateful to have some company on this awful afternoon in town. September looked straight at Annette and Sheri and then said the nicest thing she could think of. "You seem pretty normal too—for townies."

Ten dollars' worth of quarters and two chocolate shakes later Ivan followed his long shadow down the harbor ramp. "Are you sure this is what you want to do?"

September dragged a hand along the smooth metal railing. With the other she gathered her hair in from the steady wind. "Absolutely."

Ivan turned down the main harbor float leading to the *Williwaw*'s slip and the dreaded talk with Harry. An afternoon at the Dockside and a belly full of chocolate shakes was a pretty heady experience to come down from so soon. "But we can still go to TC's birthday party, right?"

"That's going to be for Dad and Harry and Aunt Nelda to decide tomorrow night." September tossed a look at the Dockside Traders, where they'd left behind TC and two unexpected new friends, Sheri and Annette. "But I hope so."

"How about if I do the talking?" Ivan looked intently, hopefully, at his sister.

September saw the big empty place beside the dock where the *Williwaw* should have been. "That would be all right with me, but I think you're going to be talking to yourself."

Ivan turned and saw that Harry wasn't there. He stood dumb alongside September, who also had a momentary lapse of plan. They'd made up their minds to stay with Harry and trust him with their predicament and it had not occurred to either of them that he might not be available to receive the honor.

"He's still up at Port Vixen, if Harry's who yer lookin' for. Fogbound 'most all day." The bent old harbor master spoke right behind their heads and gave loose a phlegmy cackle that nearly spooked Ivan and September right off the edge of the dock in surprise.

"Yer them Steamer Cove kids, ain'tcha?" He spit into the water and looked through one eye at each of them—his two eyes not quite ever pointed at the same thing.

"Y-yes, sir," September stammered. "Do you know when he'll be back?"

"Don't 'spect him till well after midnight. But no worries 'bout yer delivery—he'll be on 'is mail rounds in the morning— same as ever." The harbor master continued shuffling along the dock, his eyes and thoughts already wobbling off to the western sky.

"Red sky at night the sailors..." He hacked another throaty juicer over the rail without finishing the expression.

"How delightful." September cringed as the gnarly, aged old salt continued on his evening watch, rasping and ahoying to anyone he met.

"Aunt Nelda doesn't have a phone out at the homestead, so now what?" Ivan chirped, knowing perfectly well what.

"Don't get too cheerful," September warned even as she felt a little cheered herself. "We need to go home tonight, but this only buys us a few hours. We're still telling Harry the whole story in the morning."

"I know, but that's one more night of freedom just the same. Right?" Ivan made for the *Four-O-Five*, still tucked safely out of sight.

"If you can call it freedom." September spotted their dad's wadded coverall and hat and the buoy in the bottom of the boat and remembered. "Well, now I guess we'll have to go through with the show for Mooseburger. You know he'll be watching like a hawk when we come home."

"I know," Ivan said, regarding the setting sun. "It's perfect timing. We'll jam some wood chips in the dummy and be there right about dark."

"It better work," September said, wrestling into her gear. "We've got enough trouble without Berger getting on our case too. As long as we leave with Harry first thing, ol' Mooseburger will never know the difference."

Ivan nodded while he put the empty gas can up on the seat beside him.

"We've got just enough money left to fill that with," September said. "And just enough time. Let's go before the fuel dock closes and then hit the mill."

Ivan took two pulls on the starter cord, and the motor struggled to life while September cleared the lines from the dock. As the skiff puttered out of the calm shadows into the breeze, September studied the pile of fake-dad parts at her feet, and her heart started knocking in her chest.

Ivan peered over the side cautiously as he maneuvered toward the gas pump. "How deep you figure we are, Sep?"

September answered without looking up from her thoughts. "Over our heads, Ivan. Way over our heads."

CHAPTER 9

Ivan gripped the helm with both hands to stay properly angled in front of the lively sea following them home. He regarded the crab-pot buoy, a simple orange plastic ball strapped to the stuffed coverall resting against his sister's knees, and tried to decide if it was an approximation of their father.

"What do you think of him?" September hollered across the length of the skiff.

"Looks a little round-headed," he observed.

September punched open the floppy nor'easter and secured the hat over the buoy with the chin strap. "Better?"

Ivan looked sideways at it and nodded. Then noticing another skiff pounding into the swell toward them, he said, "Let's put it to the test."

September knew exactly what he meant and carefully dragged the dummy dad across the bottom of the boat. Together they fumbled the limp replica into a sitting position between them. September looked hard ahead at the approaching skiff.

"Nobody we know," she said, and grabbed the bulging sleeve beside her at the point where an elbow might have been.

Ivan held tight to the tiller with one hand and wrapped his other arm around the middle of their construction to steady it. "Those gloves are a nice touch. Are they going to stay on?"

September checked the twine wrapped around sleeve end and work glove to be sure no parts came undone at a critical or embarrassing moment. "All set!" she said, bracing and keeping an eye on the other boat.

"Okay, let's show them how charming this dummy can be!"

Keeping her own arms as low as she could, September raised the bogus hand into the air. Four hands in the other skiff responded to the greeting immediately, and the people returned to their conversations. It was just two boats of friendly people passing in the evening swell, eager to get home before dark.

"It worked!" September embraced the sleeve.

"Score!" Ivan slapped the knee of the dummy and returned his attention to the parade of sea swells following them home. It looked ideal for skiff surfing, thought Ivan, wringing the last bit of throttle to catch up with the face of the next wave. The *Four-O-Five* fell forward with the momentum of the sea exactly like a surfer does on a good curl.

"Woo-hoo!" they both hooted as the big guy in the middle flopped between boy and girl. The weight of the dummy against them felt right, and neither Ivan nor September made any move to return the decoy to the bottom of the boat.

The east wind blows you side to side. They sang, bouncing the dummy back and forth like a medicine ball, settling into the long ride home and trying to keep their minds on something besides tomorrow.

The west wind makes like a ride on a slide. It dawned on September that their mother's "Four Winds" song was about going home on Bag Bay. She'd always assumed it was another old sailors' rhyme like "Red Sky in Morning." She'd thought their mom had added the twist of bouncing them on her knees to entertain her children. But sitting in the quiet of her thoughts beneath the roar of the motor at her back, September could see the song was about this very route across Bag Bay. Her mother must have made up the whole thing.

September charted it in her head. Bag Bay lay almost perfectly to the north and south, and on a map looked like a big sack held open at the top. Everything on Bag Bay seemed named for what it did or what it looked like. On the right side of the sack was a little thumb of a point called Point Thumb. The crook of the thumb created a natural harbor where the town sat. On the left side of the sack stood Cape Protection, guarding the bay from the prevailing westerly winds off the Gulf of Alaska. On the bottom sides of the bag were many bulges and blisters made by the protected little coves and bights, including Steamer Cove.

The beeline they made from town to Steamer Cove ran so that an east wind blew nearly crosswise to a boat going that way and did blow you "side to side." West winds curled around Cape Protection on the northwest lip and brought long, smooth swells nearly straight down the bay like "a ride on a slide." And finally, thought September, the lush flat river valley to the south of Bag Bay cooked in the summer sun, and when a rare breeze escaped from that direction it did "mumble warm and low."

"The north wind blows you all the way home," September recalled, and turned back to witness the already darkening northern sky. She thought about the climax of the song. The north end of the bay was the open end. A wind coming from that direction would have the force of the unbridled sea behind it stuffing every bit of wind and water it could enlist right down into the sack.

September had stood with her father on the rocky Point Expectation at Steamer Cove and watched the fierce northern gales pound along the bay. Waves taller than their cabin, roof and all, sweeping by like a column of foaming demons. "Temmy, it's a fine day to be snug at home," he'd said.

Mom sang "all the way home...to me!"

The skiff scooped up a patch of sea spray and slapped September cold in the face with it, snuffing her warm thoughts and bringing her back to the Bag Bay of the moment. The sun had slipped low, leaving the mountain peaks stenciled black against a brilliant sky so red it looked sore. Wiping her face on the shoulder of the dummy dad she caught the scent of her father and tasted the sea on her lips, salty as tears. Her heart plunged along with the skiff as she remembered what they would have to tell their dad the next evening.

On the dummy's other flank, Ivan spit the salt water out of his mouth and tightened his lips, concentrating mostly on the shakes and fries sloshing around inside of him. Every jolt of the boat made him sicker. Somehow the sicker he got the more he thought of Aunt Nelda and the farm until he could hardly tell what was making him feel so bad.

Ivan continued turning downwind as they neared Steamer Cove, and the closeness of home warmed his spirits just enough to make it.

"There's Berger's place!" he called across the dummy. "What now, Sep?"

September pulled herself up, then arranged the dead weight at her side into some semblance of a posture. The dusky light was perfect, she thought—enough twilight to show three figures arriving in a boat, but not enough to make out the details—even if a telescope was involved.

"I'll handle this thing," September said, pulling her arms around the settling figure between them. "You watch out for those rocks!"

Ivan cut back only slightly on the throttle. With the sea pushing him along from behind, he needed to keep his speed up to hold control. The flooding water drew the skiff forward. Several sharp rocks stood like granite gargoyles at the mouth of the cove. Ivan gunned the engine once and skirted the first. Swinging the tiller sharply to the opposite side, he twisted the throttle again long enough to swing the *Four-O-Five*'s tail clear of the next dark crag. A third one was already invisible, lost under the rising tide, but Ivan knew that Berger's light lined up with the open channel and that's where he steered them. As if descending into the belly of the beast, Ivan aimed straight for the enemy's light before bearing off toward the Crane cabin.

Once clear of the obstacles, Ivan idled the motor down and carved a gentle sweeping arc to their dock. The motion of the current held them secure to the piling. He killed the engine.

"Nice landing, Captain," September growled in her lowest voice while pushing the sawdust arm up to a crab-buoy salute.

"Thank you, Commander Airhead." Ivan returned the

dummy's salute and stepped onto the dock to tie off. His nervous stomach relaxed as soon as his feet hit the solid planks. He took a deep breath and looked across to Berger's cabin with its faint light showing in two small windows. As he watched, one opening went dark and stayed that way.

"Mooseburger is standing in his window." Ivan looked at September, who hadn't moved from her seat beside Dummy Dad.

September, smiling like a pirate, said, "I think it's time to put on a show."

She held the dummy around the waist with one arm while the limp sleeve of saw chips rested across her shoulders. The empty head wobbled slightly as if in agreement.

"He's watching everything we do, so let's make this good." Ivan put his back to the cove and didn't move. "If you can stand straight up with dear old Dad and come toward me, I'll lift him onto the dock. To Mooseburger it will look like we're hugging."

September heaved the weight of their giant puppet up and over the side in one big movement. Ivan caught hold of the middle and wrapped his arms around it tight.

"You get under one arm, I'll take the other, and let's walk straight up to the cabin. Ready?" September directed.

"Go." Ivan set off up the dock, September keeping pace on the other side of the mock fisherman hurrying home from a long trip. The footless legs dragged slightly behind trailing sawdust on the planking.

"He's leaking," Ivan said, breathless. "And he looks dead."

"Walk faster!" September barked. "Before he drops!"

By the time they reached the shadows of the front porch, and safety from spying eyes, the sack of chips had practically slid through their grip. The now empty legs were splayed down the steps, and the nor'easter dangled from the bald head that drooped between Ivan and September like a drunken sailor.

Ivan collapsed puffing against the generator bike while September fiddled for the door latch. The door swung open with the touch of her hand, and she hesitated.

"Did we close this door?" she asked.

"It closes itself, doesn't it?"

"You have to help when it swells with this wet weather. I was the last one out this morning and I'm sure I closed it." September cast a suspicious eye at the dim windows across the cove and then dismissed the thought. "Anyway—let's get this dummy inside."

Ivan took hold of the twisted legs, and with September on the other end they hauled it into the dark cabin and over to the table. After setting the figure in their father's customary chair, they wedged it against the table and rested the arms on top of it. September lit the table lamp and stood back to admire the scene.

The lamplight shone low on the father figure sitting in the usual place at the table. The globe of a head remained above the light, leaving an impression of a family gathering around the table for an evening of cards. Ivan took his place, and the picture was complete.

September walked back onto the porch to see the effect. A large and very fatherly shadow cast its projection on the window facing Mooseburger. The flicker of the lamp made the silhouette move, and even from these few feet away the charade seemed convincing.

On the way back inside, the door swung into the light, and September froze at what she saw. "Ivan, look!"

Ivan leaned across the table and held the lamp high. "We've had company," he said somberly and brought the lamp over to the door.

"It's a bear all right." September traced a finger down one of the parallel scratches alongside the latch.

"A little one," Ivan added.

"Oh, please tell me our little bear hasn't come inside!" September moaned. "Remember what that blackie did to Aunt Nelda's last summer!"

Ivan scanned the cabin's two rooms for any signs of bear mischief—usually a mess of the foulest proportions involving food, slobber, musk, mucus, and worse. They well knew bears of any size were not dainty houseguests. Bears could rip through a cabin like a garbage bomb, so it took no more than a glance around to guess that their little bear had not come through the door.

"We're okay." He sighed. "Besides, Aunt Nelda and Uncle Spitz leave food around and that's what brings bears inside. We've never been that stupid. All our food is out in the... uh-oh."

Ivan set the lantern down on the counter beside the sink and held up an empty plastic bag and a kitchen knife. "What's this?"

September cringed. "Oops. We were in such a hurry this morning, I never cleaned up after making our sandwiches."

She rubbed her hand against the gashed door. "If that's what the bear was after, he might have come in. We'll have to close the bear boards tomorrow before we leave."

Ivan also hadn't thought to secure the big, heavy shutters on the windows and the bar over the door. These were never used for day trips away, only when they were going to be gone for a week or more. Regardless, Ivan was happy this goof-up wasn't his. He looked at the oily bag, sniffed it, and moved the light around the counter again. "There's no scraps, but it doesn't look like a bear fooled with it. There's no chew marks. It almost looks like it's been cleaned. Did you wipe this out?"

"Might have, I don't know. I was in such a hurry. Maybe the bear started in but lost his nerve. Shine the light over here." September stooped to examine the complex crisscross of foot marks imprinted on the worn floorboards. This morning's traces had already gone to dusty outlines while the fresh muddy prints glistened in the shapes of their boot soles.

There was nothing resembling a bear paw—only Ivan and September's identical-size tracks and a couple of great big dad-size treads already dried and fading. With the dummy dad looming over the table, September thought nothing of the big boot prints at first look. Then all at once it struck her that stuffed fathers without feet do not leave boot prints on the floor.

"Ivan!" She shrunk back from the print like it was a snake. "We *have* had company. And unless he wears a size eleven mud boot when he goes visiting, this is not our little bear."

Ivan squatted next to the tracks and scraped his finger through one. "Gotta be ol' Mooseburger."

"Gotta be," September agreed nervously. She stood up and looked out into the deepening night, then back to their violated home. Her heart pounded as she pictured the nasty old man poking around her private life. Ivan's bed remained a bundle of unmade blankets as he'd left it. Hers was neat and unrumpled, as she'd left it. Everything seemed in its proper place except the loose wires of the missing radios, which had lain in a tangle on the counter all week, just as they were now.

"He knows we don't have the radios," Ivan said.

CHAPTER 10

Ivan sat with his back against the dummy, sharing his chair and a deck of cards. Sticking his hands partway into the gloves he was able to wave the limp sleeves around like a marionette. September poured their tea and gave a tight little laugh, her nerves still on edge.

"That looks good, Ivan. Keep it up. I want Mooseburger good and sure Dad is home tonight."

"Dad *is* home." Ivan held the dummy's arms wide and spoke in his deepest voice, which was not very deep at all. "Bring your dear old dad his tea and sit down, Temmy."

September laughed for real and played along. "Here you go, Dad." She set Ivan's tea in front of him and sat down across the table with her own. "Tell me about your trip."

Ivan raised the cup of tea past his own mouth to the dummy head. "Ahh, that's good tea," he deadpanned. "You don't get tea like that out on the Bering Sea, by golly. Out there, why we gotta boil the bait to make our soup and give the best pieces back to the crabs."

September giggled at the perfect mockery of their dad's long tales of woe from his fishing trips. "So, did you catch some crabs and make us a lot of money?"

"Oh, there were a few crabs around, but you know we don't talk about money in this family, Temmy. We just talk about boats and fish." Then Ivan reached up with a glove and made rubbing motions on the side of the orange ball exactly the way their dad scratched his head when he wanted to change a subject. September had to snort her tea back into the cup.

"So, tell me about your week," he said, spreading the dummy's arms across the table and thoroughly enjoying commanding the stage.

September joined the act. She spoke in a mock little-girl voice. "Well, let's see...First Ivan cooked the radios right after you told him not to—that was fun! And then we decided rather than go to Aunt Nelda's where you wouldn't worry about us, we'd stay out here all by ourselves without a radio like you told us *never* to do. We got all our work done and dug eighty dollars' worth of clams in our spare time."

"How interesting," said Dummy Dad.

"Then we lied to Mr. Berger and just about everyone else we saw while we were in town where you told us not to go, and spent the afternoon drinking chocolate shakes and eating French fries over at the Dockside with some townies and a new kid from Seattle."

"I'm so proud of you!"

"I bet you are, Dad. But that's not all! We came home and found I'd left some food out, and a bear scratched up the door trying to get in, and—best of all!—mean old Mr. Berger has been snooping around the cabin, and he's across the cove right now looking at us through his telescope!"

"What could be more exciting than that?" Ivan slapped the gloves on the table.

"Oh, the fun never stops in Steamer Cove, Dad! In the morning we get to pack up our stuff and go across with Harry to see Aunt Nelda!" September's act had turned shrill, and she glared at the round hollow head as if it could see her.

Ivan tried to keep the fun going. "Well, good old Aunt Nelda and Uncle Spitz. What will you be doing there?"

September folded her arms. "You tell me, O fisher king."

Ivan pulled the gloves together and looked out between the sleeves at his sister. "I suppose you'll be dodging those two billy goats in the yard on your way to shovel the horse apples out of the barn."

"That's one thing."

"You'll be up before the crows every day to feed the chickens, gather eggs, and slop the pigs with Uncle Spitz's porcupine stew if you can get it away from him."

September was not entertained anymore. "That's three more things. Four if you count arguing with Uncle Spitz."

"Then you'll walk a mile down that muddy lane to meet the school bus and go to town school where all the kids can make fun of you and your brother for smelling like chickens, pigs, goats, and porcupine stew!"

September slammed her fist on the table, upsetting one of the mugs of tea. "Why are you making us go there?"

"I'm not." The gloves spoke quietly.

"Then who is?"

Ivan opened the arms of the dummy from in front of his face and let them fall loose.

"Your brother, Sep." Ivan spoke in his normal voice. "It's your brother made you go when he toasted the radio set."

September bit her lip. The tea spilled over the table edge, hitting the floor like hard rain. She hoisted her eyes once more to the round shadowy head above her brother's. "But why doesn't he trust us?" she squeaked, needing to know.

"He can't," Ivan said softly—knowing.

The next morning a brisk westerly wind chattered the sticks in the trees and swept pale leaves into the water. September stood beside her brother on the dock with her back to the wind. She stared absently at fresh snow capping the distant mountains.

"Winter's coming," she said.

"So's Harry." Ivan shrugged a shoulder toward the point right as the *Williwaw* slid from beyond the boulders and turned sharply into the channel.

"Are you ready for this?" September asked.

"No," Ivan said.

Harry worked the big wheel hard to one side and then the other to clear the entrance rocks. The *Williwaw*'s stack belched black smoke while Harry reversed the engine and powered against the surging tide. With an expert throw of the wheel the bow came around and the tough wood boat eased to the dock. Harry stepped on deck just in time to slide a rubber bumper between boat and dock to save his paint job.

"I love it when the magic works! Har har har!" Harry tossed Ivan a line. "Tie 'er off, Captain, an' a Bag Bay good mornin' to you, Little Miss!" Harry handed September a short stack of mail tied with a string.

"Hi, Harry," said Ivan.

"Hi, Hairy," said September.

Harry cocked one eye at the glum pair on the dock. "You two look about as cheerful as a toothache. What's goin' on over here? I haven't heard nothin' from you on the radio all week."

The kids were silent, and Harry cleared his throat as he sighted down his nose at them. "Methinks there's somethin' to those rumors I been hearin' in town."

Harry had Ivan's and September's full attention now as he continued. "Some yappy kid wearin' his pop's trousers knocked on my hatch first thing this mornin' lookin' for you."

"TC," Ivan moaned. His breath came out in a long steamy cloud, and he hunkered into his coat.

"That's 'is name," Harry said. "He was headin' off to school, an' wanted to know where you was. I said you was across, an' he said ya weren't, an' you was comin' to some party, an' I said you'd never go against yer pop like that and come to town, but he said ya did, an' now I'm thinkin' ya did—didn'tcha?"

"Twice, Harry. We went across twice." September fingered the mail in her hands.

Harry's head slowly wobbled back and forth on his shoulders. "That sure explains why you haven't called me for groceries. Yer probably fulla them Frenchy fries and malteds. That it?"

September straightened up as best she could under the weight of what she had to say. "We don't need groceries, but that's not why you haven't heard from us. We didn't call because our radio doesn't work. We had to take it to town for repairs."

Harry's head nodded on top of wobbling and was nearly turning circles. "I was wonderin' when you'd tell me 'bout that. Yer

106

chatty friend gave me the whole story." Harry looked hard at September.

"Two kids across the bay by themselves with no radio!" He turned to Ivan. "An' I don't suppose that little video rig-a-jig of yours had anything to do with it?"

"Everything," Ivan said. "Don't blame Sep. It's all my fault."

September disagreed. "I went along with the whole thing, Harry. We should have come straight to you."

"Yes, you should've. I told your pop I'd look after you. *Holy herring and mother of cod,* he'd have me *pickled* if anything happened to you kids!" Harry looked from one to the other, his big hands balled on his hips and his face the color of the reddest checks on his shirt.

"We're sorry, Harry," September said. "We'll go with you right now and we'll use your radio to tell Dad everything when he calls tonight. We've got all our stuff together to stay with Aunt Nelda. Can you drive us out there?"

"Exactly what I plan to do! We'll get goin' just as soon as Berger gets over here for his delivery." The kids followed Harry's gaze across the cove to see Mr. Berger climbing into his rowing dinghy.

September twirled back to Harry and seized him by the cuff. "Oh, Harry, there's one more thing we have to tell you, and we need your help!"

Harry sat heavily on the hatch cover as September gushed out the story of old Mooseburger's threats and the dummy dad up in the cabin. She insisted Berger couldn't find out it was a hoax. He'd been sneaking around the cabin and would surely call the authorities if he knew they'd been left alone this long without even a radio to call for help.

Mooseburger was close enough that they could hear his oars squeaking in their oarlocks. "Awright," Harry finally said. "I'll go along with it. But only 'cause yer pop worries about that old coot an' I don't trust him either! Not any further'n I could spit." With that he did spit, and as if to make his point, it landed right on top of his boot.

"What's an old man gotta do to get some mail service around here!" Berger's puckered face appeared over the opposite rail.

"Good mornin', Berger." Harry wiped his beard and manufactured a bright smile through the thick of it.

"Ain't either a good morning. It's a cold morning," Berger grouched.

Harry fetched a box from under the hatch. "Yep, the season's turned on us. Maybe you better hurry back to that warm cabin of yours," he said.

"I will!" Berger snapped. "But not until I have a word with the father of these two hooligans here! Caught them on my beach stealing clams you know!"

"Oh, you did now? Maybe we oughta shoot 'em!" Harry teased.

"I thought of that." Berger spoke without a trace of humor. He pulled himself and the dinghy around the bow of the *Williwaw* and took hold of a dock piling. "Now let me see that so-called father of yours!"

Ivan stuttered for a moment before September found her tongue. "He's sick and still sleeping. And Harry's going to take us all to town as soon as he wakes up. Right, Harry?"

"Sure. Just as soon as he wakes up."

Berger put a hand out and swept up some of the sawdust and wood chips on the planking. "What kind of sick is he? Seasick?"

"Yeah, that's it!" Ivan blurted without thinking. "I mean, no! He's, uh, land sick! He's been at sea so long he got sick as soon as he hit the dock! Right, Harry?"

Harry cocked his head the way a dog will at a boat whistle and could find nothing to say that might support the notion. He simply nodded dumbly and widened his eyes at Ivan.

"Hooey!" Berger dismissed it and glared straight at September. The black centers of his eyes were clouded in a way that left a chilled pit in her middle. He growled on. "Yer ol' man didn't look none too steady when he came home last night. I'd say he's sleepin' off a drunk is what he's doin'!"

September bristled, and her eyes flared right back at Berger. "Our dad doesn't drink, and you know it!"

"Where's he at then?" The old man filtered sawdust through his fingers into the water.

"We told you, he's sick in bed." Ivan felt an odd sensation to be passionately defending the honor of a father made up primarily of loose dust and spare clothing.

Berger put one foot on the dock but made no move to follow it. He brushed his hands on the raised knee and addressed Harry. "I hope their father has the sense to clean up the garbage and close the bear boards before he goes."

Harry said nothing. Ivan focused on Mooseburger's big muddy boot and the words leaped from him. "Maybe we oughta close the nosy old man boards, too!" He scowled.

Berger just glowered and reached into his grubby coat pocket.

"And maybe *you* oughta thank an old man for lookin' after you!" He threw a handful of smoked fish and skin scraps onto the dock. "I saw that pesky little bear poking around on your porch yesterday afternoon, an' I come over to see what he was after."

Berger stabbed at the evidence with the toe of his boot. "You careless kids are gonna teach that bear bad habits and then it'll have to be shot!"

Harry finally spoke up. "You got a problem bear runnin' around here?"

"He's a sweet little bear!" September insisted. "I left food out by accident. It wasn't his fault. He was just being a bear."

Harry considered for a moment, then pointed a big finger at Berger. "In that case, I think ya owe Mr. Berger an apology. Sounds to me like he did you a neighborly turn."

The prospect of gratitude drove Berger to his oars quicker than any threat or insult could have. "I don't want that bear learnin' there's benefit to breaking into cabins." He pushed off from the dock. "An' I still want to see that father of yours. If he can *pull himself* together."

"Okay, Mr. Berger," Ivan said too nicely. "As soon as we get back."

Berger huffed away without another word. Harry waved him off and leaned over to Ivan and September.

"I don't think he believes your dad is in the house," he whispered.

"You weren't much help," Ivan said.

Harry waited to speak until Berger was well away. "I guess I'm not as good a liar as some."

September shifted her feet. Ivan studied a thread hanging from his sleeve.

"I don't wanna be around when your pop hears of all this," Harry finally said.

"But we need to use your radio tonight when he calls," Ivan fretted.

"That's fine," Harry allowed. "I'm just not going to be there for the fireworks."

"Well," September said, "we should go."

Harry held up his hands. "Not so fast there, Little Miss. Don'tcha think Berger made his point? Ya better get them bear boards closed up and barricade your other supplies, or your pop might come home to find one heckuva big mess and nothin' for his supper either."

"You're right. We're just not used to thinking of our little bear as trouble."

"Then ya better start." Harry faced the cabin. "How long'll it take ya to button 'er up?"

"Hours," Ivan said tiredly. "The boards don't fit right, and we have to screw each one of them in by hand."

Harry reached into his coat and after some fumbling produced a battered pocket watch. "Oh, jeez. Now that's a problem. I'm behind on my deliveries on accounta that fog yesterday kept me up at Port Vixen all the darn day."

Harry chewed one end of his mustache and looked out at the bay rolling by in the long even swells of a light west wind. He eyed the *Four-O-Five* and scratched under his cap. He looked at the cabin. And then at the kids. And at Berger just making shore on the other side. He snorted a couple of fog streams out his nose, saying cautiously, "The weather out there's supposed to hold. Ya think ya can get yourselves across it one more time?"

"Of course we can!" September said, happy to have Harry's faith again.

Harry spoke like a captain. "You get squared away out here an' make your way to the harbor. I'll feed ya supper an' you can talk with your pop an' bunk on the *Williwaw* tonight, if that's okay with him. We'll go on out to your aunt's in the morning."

"After the party?" Ivan gambled the question.

"Don't ask me. Ask your pop," Harry commanded as he twisted the tie line loose. He reached into the pilothouse for the control and dropped the *Williwaw* into reverse. The quietly pounding diesel lugged down slightly and the prop wash bubbled in the widening gulf between boat and kids.

"I'll be at the harbor by five this afternoon." Harry's forehead was creased in a very unhappy manner. "You better be too."

"Trust us!" September managed a smile.

"I do," Harry said, but not loud enough to offer any comfort to the sorry pair left on the dock.

CHAPTER 11

Late that afternoon when the work was done, Ivan ducked inside the cabin. He tossed a short piece of cord to September, who sat on the floor alongside the stuffed dummy. "These'll do the job. We'll walk 'Dad' between us straight to the boat."

"This is the most ridiculous idea you've ever had, Ivan." September snatched the cord out of the air and used it to tie one leg of the dummy dad to her ankle. "But I think it might actually work."

Ivan secured his own foot to the other side. "It's the best we can do in broad daylight. As long as we move fast, Mooseburger will never be able to focus on us with his telescope." Ivan peeked out the door. Nothing was stirring on the breeze-rippled cove. "Are we good to go?"

September made one last mental survey. Their packs, filled with school clothes and some homegrown food offerings for Aunt Nelda, were already in the skiff. They'd scrubbed out all the pans and cupboards for insurance against the bear and then drained the water in the cabin to keep the pipes from freezing up if it turned very cold before they returned. The bear boards were all in place and the door bolt ready to secure. The root cellar was barricaded and nailed shut as well. They'd beached the *Aunt Nelda* and turned it bottom side up in the tall grass.

Satisfied that the place could be left for a week or so, September clutched the dummy by the shoulder and lifted it into view. "Ready when you are."

Ivan hefted his share of the load, and the three of them waltzed awkwardly out into the light. Ivan pulled the door closed. September dropped the heavy wooden bar into place.

"Let's go!" she said, and off they went down the trail as if they were running a three-legged race. With the dummy's legs attached to their own, the phony father figure appeared to stride along the dock between them with a somewhat clumsy but convincing ease.

When they jumped into the *Four-O-Five*, the dummy flopped onto the seat and whiplashed its hat off. Ivan captured the nor'easter and drew it back over the orange ball. "I'll get this, Sep. You get us out of here."

September set her ankle free and stood to prime the motor. Looking anxiously over at Berger's place, she suddenly saw a puff of white smoke near his porch, and then a heartbeat later she heard the crack of a gunshot. Both kids instinctively ducked below the dock and stared wildly at each other, their eyes asking, *Is he shooting at us?*

The unspoken question was quickly answered when they heard an eerily human sound pierce the day like a baby's wail. "Our little bear!" they cried, and stood to see a patch of black tearing up the northern hillside. They listened, but the wailing stopped.

"He missed," Ivan said, breathing again.

"How do you know?"

"If Mooseburger'd hit him with that blaster he calls a rifle, the little bear couldn't have charged up the hill like he did. And he's stopped bawling. He was scared, that's all. He's halfway to Huckleberry Cove by now."

"Oh, I hope so." September looked from the ridge to Mr. Berger climbing up the steps to his cabin.

"The little bear is helping to distract Berger to cover our escape," she said.

"Now *that's* a good bear," Ivan replied. "We better get on with the show before Mooseburger finds the way back to his telescope."

Ivan undid his ankle tether and arranged the dummy's legs. September primed the fuel line and was balancing herself to pull the starter cord when a thought occurred to her.

"Ivan, if the bear is helping us get away today, then why do you suppose it tried to get into the cabin yesterday?"

"Maybe it wanted us to stay home," he said, looking out the mouth of the cove to the white-capped swells licking at the rocks. He knew it was going to be a long rough ride to town, but they'd been in much worse. Ivan dismissed the subject. "He probably just wanted some lunch. Who can tell?"

September turned her attention to the weather. The two young eagles stood almost motionless in the sky as they hovered over the beach in the persistent wind. The swells rolled by, round and steady. "It's a day breeze and will only get better as the sun goes down."

"Unlike the rest of our lives," Ivan complained.

"We can always hope Dad will let us go to TC's party tomorrow morning before Harry takes us out to Aunt Nelda's. But I doubt it." September pulled the starter and the skiff quivered beneath them.

Ivan untied the lines and pushed clear of the dock. "Me too. We'll be lucky if Dad doesn't have us led away in shackles and chains."

September said nothing, looking wistfully at their boarded-up cabin while buckling her life jacket. She handed Ivan his, then straightened her course. The tide was at high ebb, so the mouth of the cove was wide and deep and the day swells jammed in against the sentry rocks. The light skiff pitched and bucked on its way through the agitated water. Ivan finished fastening his gear while momentarily forgetting to support the madly flopping rag-doll dad.

The first swell catapulted the dummy headfirst into the bottom of the boat. Ivan and September each got a hand on it and launched it back into position on the seat with such a force that the head fell completely off and bounced around loosely at their feet. Ivan chased it with his hands, finally pouncing upon it like a football player recovering a fumble.

"Got it!"

"Hurry and tie it on." September pushed the dummy down and looked back at the cove. "We're still in Berger's sights."

Ivan grabbed one of the scraps of line they'd used for the three-legged waddle. Reaching inside the neck cavity of the dummy, he found the loop that had come undone and quickly fastened the orange ball back in place with the new cord. "That should hold it!"

Together they heaved the lop-headed dummy back to its seat and pressed on into the bay.

"Do you think Mooseburger saw?" September said, making herself not look back again.

"We're moving around so much it could've looked like Dad bent down to work on the gas tanks or something. We'll be out of range soon enough." Ivan ducked as sea spray came up from the bow in a rooster tail. The wind caught it and slapped them across the faces with cold disregard.

"It's going to be uphill all the way to town," Ivan said, spitting seawater and cinching his hood down as tight as it would go.

September closed her hood and then borrowed the dummy's hat to put on top of that. They would have to beat into the wind and swell until they reached the harbor. It was her least favorite kind of trip across. It wasn't dangerous—the trusty *Four-O-Five* was well-built to handle just such a condition—but it was annoying.

Each rising swell would pick up the pointed bow, and then as it passed under the boat, plunge it into the face of the next swell, scooting Ivan and September slightly forward on their rumps and hosing them with water. After an hour of this, every leak in their rain gear would be discovered and their hind ends would be tenderized.

By the middle of the bay, when the winds had started to fall off as September had predicted, she still made no adjustments to their speed. The swells were more gentle and the spray far less punishing, and it felt good to ride the lazy roller coaster of it with the last of the summer wind lightly in her face.

The glaciers on the east side of the bay spilled between the mountain peaks like melting vanilla ice cream. It was a sweet image to have in all the salt air and cooled the bile starting to burn in the pit of her stomach as the harbor flags came solidly into focus.

"Right on time," September said without pride as she grappled inside her sleeve to check her watch.

As she made the turn toward the harbor opening, Ivan folded the dummy dad down out of view. Lying there with its sawdust limbs crossed over themselves, it looked like a circus freak doing contortions in the bottom of the boat. "The harbor master won't know *what* to think if he sees this."

They both laughed for only as long as it took them to round the harbor wall and see the *Williwaw* tied in its usual slip.

"I guess this is it then." Ivan shed his gear and draped the jacket over the dummy like a shroud. September dropped the hat over that.

"Rest in peace, Airhead."

September motored to their usual place. They had no reason to hide anymore, but this berth had proved to be secure as well as secret, and neither she nor Ivan knew when they might be back for the *Four-O-Five*. They stowed everything as best they could under the seats and swung the two sturdy canvas packs onto the dock.

They shouldered their loads for the short walk to Harry's boat slip. Above their heads, on the ramp to the street, a loud commotion startled them. Seagulls scattered, trailing insults, and TC suddenly appeared at the bottom of the ramp in a streak of nylon and denim. He stomped one end of his skateboard and it end-over-ended right into his waiting grip.

"Hi, Ivan! Hi, September! I saw you come in!" TC stood before them, all teeth and suntan and obviously glad to see them. "I've been looking everywhere for you!"

"Yeah. Harry told us all about it. Thanks a lot," September said accusingly.

TC looked stricken. "Did I tell him something I shouldn't have?"

"No, not really." September softened her tone. "I just wish he'd heard it from us first."

"Don't sweat it," Ivan added, and they walked together toward Harry's boat.

As they went, Ivan explained what had happened when they couldn't find Harry the night before, and how they'd had to spend the day closing up the cabin to keep the little bear out.

"There was a bear in your house?" TC was agape. "Did you shoot it?"

"No!" September snapped, then took two steps to recover her composure. "I'm sorry. It's a long story, and we're a little jumpy about guns and bears today. We've had a rough ride over, and, well, it's been a long week."

TC gave a sympathetic look. Then a crafty grin came across his face. "Hey, why don't you guys drop your stuff with that big hairy guy and I'll buy you both a shake at the Dockside." He turned and swatted Ivan playfully on his sore behind. "What d'ya say to some Tech Patrol, Dan'l Boone?"

Ivan rubbed his rear, and September's temper caved for good.

"You just don't get it, do you, guys? We're supposed to be at Harry's right now to wait for Dad's call. We're going to be in *big trouble* after that. We may lose our Dockside privileges forever, for all I know, and it's all because of *video games!*"

TC stopped in his tracks. "Does this mean you won't come to my party tomorrow?"

He still doesn't get it, thought September, but she said nothing. Ivan answered with a shrug.

"But you *have* to be there!" TC pleaded.

TC's plea was genuine, and even though September couldn't understand why he cared so much about her and Ivan being there, she flushed with the compliment of it.

"We'll ask," she said hopelessly. "That's all I can say."

"That's enough for me!" TC recovered his good cheer and dropped the skateboard beside the *Williwaw*. "Don't forget: ten o'clock!" And with that, he jumped on the board and kicked off down the harbor walk.

"And—free video games!" he crowed just before sweeping out of sight.

"Drown me, Sep." Ivan rolled his pack over the railing, and it landed with a thud on Harry's deck. "I promise I won't even struggle."

"Only if I can drown Mr. Happy with you." September threw her pack over as well. "But let's stay positive. Maybe Dad will let us go."

"Right, and maybe Aunt Nelda got rid of the pigs and put in a hot tub."

Just then Harry came up from the boat cabin. "There's them bush-rat *bandidos*! Hullo, Cap'n. Good evenin', Little Miss."

"Hello, Harry."

"'Evening, Hairy."

"Don't hang those faces so low to my decks—you'll get your lips dirty! Har har har!" Harry grabbed a pack in each hand and started down the hatchway. "I've got just the thing to put a smile back on those mugs—*boiled codfish!* C'mon down and taste the nectar. Nectar of the cods! Har har har!"

September climbed aboard stone-faced and put out a helping hand to Ivan, who stood there more miserable than ever.

"Drown me—please?" he mouthed.

September ignored him and went down the stairs, letting her own bad mood drown itself in a cloud of boiled cod vapor.

Ivan and September had never heard Harry speak of being a cook. Sitting at the galley table of the *Williwaw*, staring at their rapidly cooling meals, they now knew why. Dipping into a single kettle simmering on the stove, Harry had loaded each plate with possibly the most unappealing dinner they had ever seen. Bright white chunks of Pacific cod floated alongside pale white onions knocking around like marbles with pasty white potatoes. To Ivan it looked like the kind of food they would serve at insane asylums.

September used her fork to roll an onion through an obstacle course of cod. "Do you always cook everything in the same pot?"

"It's the only pot I got!" Harry beamed. "Works good, don't it?"

September stabbed the onion and it collapsed. Harry finally noticed they had not touched their food and smiled kindly.

"Nervous 'bout talkin' to your pop?"

Although that was only part of it, September was happy to have an excuse not to eat Harry's food. "Yes," she said, pushing away her plate.

Ivan did the same and looked at his sister's watch. "Shouldn't we have the radio on? It's almost ten till eight."

"That we should," Harry agreed, pulling himself up from the bench. "And I b'lieve I will go walk off my dinner while you an' your pop talk things over."

Ivan winced at the wall of static that filled the cabin when Harry switched on the set.

"Tell your pop I'll run you up to your aunt's first thing tomorrow. You'll bunk here in the galley tonight."

The boat swayed slightly when Harry stepped off onto the dock. Ivan eyed the hissing radio. "Who's going to do the talking?"

September's gaze funneled out the porthole above the table and focused on a pair of seagulls. They were on the harbor master's roof tugging at each end of a fish skin.

"I will," she said, and her next breath came to her in shudders as the radio barked the familiar call sign.

"Steamer Cove, Steamer Cove, this is WFX98 Marine Operator. Are you with us, kids?"

September reached for the microphone and took another breath before speaking. "Roger. This is WBN6408 Steamer Cove. Go ahead."

It was an automatic thing to say, and it didn't occur to her until she'd said it out loud that it was untrue. They were aboard the *Williwaw*, and this was Harry's radio and call sign, not theirs—although the operator and their dad could not know that from their end of the conversation. Ivan looked at September, then both looked away.

"I'll put you through, Steamer Cove. Stand by," the operator said.

Several agonizing moments passed, and then the voice of their father poured into the boat like fireweed honey.

CHAPTER 12

"Hi, Temmy, Ivan. I knew you'd be there," he said, not sounding so sure they would be.

"Hi, Dad," September chirped so pleasantly that Ivan winced and stayed silent.

"You kids all right out there?"

September pulled her shoulders back and readied herself. Ivan dropped his face onto the backs of his hands on the galley table. "We're fine, Dad, but there're some things we need to tell you about." September released the mike to gather her courage and her dad broke in.

"Are you hurt?" he asked with worried impatience.

"No, it's nothing like that. We're..." Again she had to search for the words.

"Sick? Are you sick?" he interrupted.

"No, Dad, we're fine, but—"

"Don't tell me you're hungry! You have food, don't you?"

"Yes, yes, we're fine." September was now the impatient one, but her dad seemed satisfied.

"Good. Now, I'm sure you both have lots of adventures to tell me, and I want to hear all about them, but first I want to say how proud I am of you."

Their dad's voice caught and they heard him start to clear his throat before the static resumed. September used the moment to cut in. "Dad, it's nothing like you think..."

Again she hesitated and again Mr. Crane took over. "It's more than you know, Temmy. We've really hit the crab big out here, and I'm sure that a year from now we'll be sitting on the brand-new *Mrs Crane*, telling sea stories. I have the two of you to thank for it. I don't know how I ever could have put this trip together if I couldn't trust you to look after yourselves like this."

Ivan rolled his eyes and wondered what his sister was going to do. September wondered the same thing but didn't have to decide just then.

Their dad's voice settled to a deeper tone, sounding near and comfortable like he did around their table at the cove when he lay back at the end of a long day.

"So you got the garden in?"

"Yes, but—"

"The smokehouse?"

"Mmm-hmm, although—"

"And you dug the new latrine?"

September reverted to the shorthand signal and simply keyed the mike for agreement. *Click.*

"We'll get the outhouse moved over when I get there."

"We did it already!"

"No fooling? You hardly need your old man around there anymore!" Their dad's laugh sounded like a familiar drumbeat, easy to step to. "I bet you even dug my butter clams for me!"

Ivan sat upright, amazed. September was all smiles now. "Not as many as we wanted, because ol' Moosebur—uh...I mean, the ground meat ran us off."

"Don't you bother yourself over that, honey. I'll be home soon enough. Just try to stay clear of it. We won't have ground meat or rowboat farms to concern ourselves with once we have the *Mrs Crane*. Won't that be great?"

Click.

There was a pause, and through the softer static Ivan and September could hear loudspeakers in the background. They pictured their father squeezed into the phone booth in front of the Dutch Harbor fish plant with the heel of one big hand pushed over an ear, the phone receiver pressed into the other.

"I miss you kids so much," he said, and there was more throat clearing.

Click.

September's lip trembled. Ivan coughed.

"I want you to do one more thing for me." Their dad had changed his tone along with the subject. He sounded as if he were announcing the next game of cards around the kitchen table.

"Anything," September said. Ivan waited.

"Promise me you'll be right beside the radio tomorrow. I have a surprise for you."

September looked helplessly at her brother, who pointed at the mike, meaning "Are you going to tell him or what?"

September held the mike in both hands. "Dad, there's something we want to tell you about."

"And there's so much I want to tell you about. Let's do it tomorrow." The voice still sounded untroubled and firm. "Right now—tell me what you see out the window."

September looked through the porthole at the two seagulls sitting on their roof peak clueless as a pair of wooden ducks. She saw her brother watching her with the same expression, and she made up her mind. Curling her hands tighter around the microphone, she began the story.

"I see our two loons drifting in the current off the end of the dock." She closed her eyes to avoid looking at Ivan's, which were bugged in disbelief. "The sky is barely lighter than the mountains. They look like the ghosts of mountains instead of the real deals. Berger's lantern is the brightest thing we see." September again looked at her brother, who had returned his face to the tabletop. "Except for our reflections in the windowpanes—sitting by the fire, steaming mugs of rose-hip tea in our hands—talking to you."

The static washed like the actual ocean that stood between them and their dad. Then their dad closed the distance.

"Thanks, Temmy. That was a fine tour. I've got to get off this line. There are fishermen backed up all the way to the street waiting for the phone. I just want to tell you how proud I am of you and Ivan for keeping your promises to me. Ivan, you're pretty quiet tonight, but I know you're there. I love you and I miss you both. Talk to you tomorrow. Good night."

The marine operator's voice suddenly sprang into the boat with them. "This is WFX98, and we're clear."

The radio noise blitzed from ocean waves to a wave of interference. September reached over and slowly faded it down, then off, almost afraid to be left in the quiet again. Ivan looked at his sister as one would any unexpected and totally absurd development—such as returning home to find all the furniture screwed to the ceiling and a cat serving biscuits and tea.

"Don't look at me like that," September said, wondering what in the world she'd done.

Ivan kept looking at her like that. The whole earth seemed turned around.

"I tried to tell him. I just couldn't." September absently pulled at the neck of her sweatshirt. She felt torn between the girl she'd always been and the girl who just coolly told a bald-faced lie to her father.

"What do we do about Harry?" Ivan asked.

September let loose her shirt collar, and the snap of it seemed to gather her together. "We'll tell him the truth," she fearlessly declared.

"The truth of *what* now, Little Miss?" One of Harry's slick black boots appeared on the steep stair, and the rest of him descended after. He stooped under the low ceiling and loomed directly over Ivan and September at the table. "How bad was it?"

"It wasn't bad at all," September replied, scooting over so Harry could have a seat.

"Can ya stay the night here or did he send ya straight to your aunt's?"

"Actually"—September paused to phrase her answer carefully—"he said he wanted us over at the cabin with the radios by tomorrow afternoon."

"You're pullin' on my leg!" Harry closed one eye and fixed Ivan with the other. "This the truth, Captain?"

"That's what he said, all right." Ivan saw how this could work without lying and he managed a smile at his sister. "Dad said he had a surprise for us and to be standing by the radio in the cove."

"What did he say about ya comin' back and forth on the bay an' all?"

September threw off the question with a shrug. "He never mentioned it. He was just happy to hear we'd done all the chores and brought the garden in."

"Well, pinch my finger in a ten-ton winch!" Harry tugged his beard, possibly to keep his disbelieving head still. "I'da bet the *Williwaw* herself you kids'd be on your pop's poop deck over this. Just goes to show what a mail-boat captain knows 'bout raisin' children."

"Goes to show…" Ivan agreed lamely.

"Sure does," September said.

Harry's hand went from pulling his beard to scratching at his chin. "I guess you're stayin' on board tonight, an' then back to Steamer Cove in the *Four-O-Five* until your pop comes home next week. That it, then?"

"That's it." September spoke to the table.

"Well then, let's get this galley cleaned up so ya got a place to bunk down! Let me see, I did the dishes last night an' the six hundred nights 'fore that. So I guess it's your turn! Har har har!"

Harry's laugh was far too big for this little space. It boomed in Ivan's and September's ears and out the doors and spooked two clueless seagulls off their peak. They careened through the harbor and out toward the bay with the last of the lackluster swells.

"The weather map for north Gulf waters for Saturday, September twenty-first, shows a low-pressure system building east of Kodiak Island. Forecast for Port Vixen to Point Thumb is southwest winds building to twenty knots in the morning, changing to northeast by afternoon. A gale warning is in effect for the Port Vixen vicinity Saturday afternoon through early Sunday morning…"

"Hoo-boy! They're gonna get clobbered up at Port Vixen again." Harry lay on his bunk reading a comic book while he listened to the marine weather report. Ivan and September leaned over a pile of magazines at the table. Harry pointed at the radio and September turned it off.

"Thank you, Little Miss. That's about all the entertainment I can stand. You kids'll wanna get straight across in the mornin'. That sou'wester won't hurt a thing inside the bay—just a chop, I 'spect. But don' let that nor'easter get near ya." Harry rolled up on one elbow to be sure his guests were listening. "When she comes northeast in September, most anything can happen. That's williwaw weather."

"Why does that happen?" Ivan asked.

"Williwaw? It happens when a storm gets bottled up behind those mountains." Harry pointed in the general direction of the range of white peaks behind the town. "Pretty soon it spills over into the narrow little glacier valleys an' such, and it's like punchin' a hole in a tire. All that air comin' through one little place makes for one heckuva blowout! I've seen the forest laid down flat for a mile. Williwaws took down many a good boat and crew. Horrid, awful things. Took down your mother, one did."

Harry didn't seem to know what he'd said until he heard it himself. Then the little bit of skin that showed on his face turned pink. "I'm sorry to mention that," he managed.

September forgave the embarrassed skipper with a smile. "It's okay, Harry."

Ivan swung around on his bench. "Dad doesn't like to talk about it."

"No," Harry said, "that's true enough. He don't."

"Why is that?" Ivan asked.

Harry thought on it. Some of the bigness seemed to leak out of him, and he laid the comic book aside. Finally he said, "I think a big part of your pop went down with your mother an' that boat. He don't talk to nobody about it. An' I never heard him call your mother anything 'cept 'Mrs. Crane' since. Like he can't even bear to say 'er name out loud."

"Adrietta," September said.

"Adrietta," Harry repeated. "A lovely name for a lovely lady. I think your pop misses her like sweet water."

"Tell us, Harry," Ivan said. "Tell us what really happened that night. Do you remember?"

Harry looked from one to the other and said, "Was a night I will not forget."

He continued. "Seems half the people on Bag Bay was down with flu that September. Adrietta, your mother, had took the *Adrietta*, your fishin' boat, to town after your uncle called to say

131

poor Aunt Nelda was scary sick. You kids was little ones, an' no sooner had your mother gone than one or both a' you come down with the sickness too. Your pop was at the cove with you an' radioed your mother to hurry home soon's she could. 'Okay,' she says, 'soon's Nelda's fever breaks,' she says."

Harry laid his head back down and spoke to the ceiling. "It was a gorgeous day. Purty as they come. But there was somethin' big an' ugly hidin' behind them mountains. I was lyin' here jus' like this. Sicker than a dirty sock myself an' listenin' to the whole thing come on. The weather turned bad faster'n you could think. By dark the wind was up my riggin', howlin' like banshees. An' that was right here in the protected harbor! The seas musta been ten to fifteen feet comin' down the bay. Your pop kept callin' for the *Adrietta* on the radio. He was gonna tell 'er stay put in town, but the signal was breakin' up bad from the storm. I picked up and hollered to your pop it was nasty town-side and nobody would take their boat out into that. This bay is a hungry, powerful critter, and she feeds on the careless and the ignorant. Your mother was neither of those."

Harry sat up again, animated by his own story. "And then I hear her through the noise—barely. She says she's under way an' comin' home to her babies."

Ivan and September sat like stone figures in the shadows, staring at the near distance.

"Your pop kep' callin' for her to turn back to port, but I had a hard time hearin' him, an' I was in my quiet bunk. Can't imagine she heard a thing out in the storm. He called over and over, 'Go back, go back, go back,' until the radio fuzzed out. Then

132

there was just the wind and the static noise for the longest time."

Harry, the tough old sailor who'd told the tales of a hundred different souls lost at sea, looked up as if to see through the roof of the boat, his face twisted in real pain. "I heard the williwaw comin' down off them mountains like a steam shovel on wings. I laid right here where you see me as parts of the old fish company warehouse was bouncin' off my decks an' the lines of every boat in the harbor was squealin' like dogs tryin' to get untied."

Harry piled his head into his beard and chest and rocked side to side as if in that wind on that night. "That's when I knew," he said, and found a calmer tone and position.

"We all went out, of course, Coast Guard, everybody—soon's the storm passed. Looked all the next day—as beautiful and flat a day on Bag Bay as ever there was—but there was no sign of either Adrietta.

"Your pop found the radio antenna blowed down behind your cabin, and he knew that's why she couldn't hear him. Blames himself still. He thinks he shoulda done a better job with your radio setup. That's why he's so crazy about the ones you got. That big battery bank an' your bicycle rig. Nothin' else like it round here."

Harry raised a hand in sudden alarm. "Now, I'm not tryin' to say nothin' bad against your pop! No, sir! Best radio set from Huckleberry Cove to Port Vixen, by gosh! That's why I can't hardly imagine him sendin' you back across after ya broke it."

Ivan, alarmed, looked at his sister for some explanation, but September wasn't ready for the practicalities of radios or alibis. She was still lost in the sweet spot of the story.

"Mom was coming home to be with us," she said quietly.

"That's a fact," Harry said, and fell back onto his pillow, biting off a yawn.

"Did you see the orca in the cove that day?" September asked while Ivan gathered up the extra blankets from under the bunk.

Harry smiled with his eyes closed. "You remember that, do ya, Little Miss? I s'pose we all do. Three times it swam by the dock and give a blow every time. One for each of you, an' off it went."

"What do you think it was?" September probed.

"I think it was a whale," Harry said flatly.

"What," she persisted, "do you think it really was?"

Harry rolled his back to the galley and hauled on his blankets. "I really do think it was a whale, Little Miss. Now good night to you both."

Harry clicked off his bunk light as Ivan tossed a blanket to September. They squirmed around on each of the galley benches to find the least punishing places among the lumpy cushions.

"Good night, Harry."

"'Night, Harry."

"Mmm."

There was nothing but the sound of little breaths and big breaths falling into pace with each other and then Ivan's voice cut the rhythm. "Harry?"

"Mmm?"

"Why did you name your boat after something so terrible?"

A long groan came from the bunk, and the whole boat moved just a little as Harry changed his position. The silence lasted so long Ivan began to think Harry had gone to sleep, but apparently he'd only been deciding how to answer.

"An old seaman once said to me to name a boat for the thing ya fear the most. *Williwaw* is that thing for me."

Again there was silence while the answer was considered.

"But what about the *Mrs Crane?*" Ivan asked.

"And the *Adrietta?*" added September.

Harry swallowed once.

"Or miss the most," he finally said, rolling back the way he was. "And sometimes they are the same thing."

Ivan pulled his blanket tight around his neck and listened to his heartbeat squish-squishing in his ear.

"I miss Dad," he said, and his heart pumped like a fever half through the night.

CHAPTER 13

September entered the galley from the deck above with her cheeks flushed rose red from the chill harbor morning. Her face seemed to borrow its color from the sky behind her in the hatchway.

"What a perfect morning!" she declared.

Harry and Ivan, absorbed in a cartoon on television, said nothing.

September placed the breakfast plates she'd finished cleaning on the counter with a racket that could not be ignored. Harry switched off the set and Ivan huffed a complaint from the galley table before turning to notice the light of day glowing red as fire.

"Wow!" he said. "Red sky in the morning, the sailors take warning."

"It's 'sailors' *hearts warming*'!" September said, opening the tired old argument. She turned to the yawning sea captain in the bunk and added, "Isn't that right, Harry?"

Harry looked out at the morning and grinned. "In most oceans, the Captain would be the right one, Little Miss. A red sky in the mornin' tells ya a front is comin' yer way, and a sailor should pay attention. A red sky at night can mean the worst is over, and it is a sailor's delight to ever think that!"

"How about around here?" she asked.

"Round here, now, that can get complicated. The weather on our coast don't always move in regular ways, see. In summer a red sky in the mornin' can mean a weather change. But in the wintertime the winds turn around by an' large. A red sky in the mornin' generally happens after a night storm, an' as ya said, that warms a sailor's heart."

"But there was no storm last night and the sky is red as ever," Ivan observed.

"That's 'cause it's September." Harry lay back and reached for the television knob again. "In the month of yer sister's namesake ya never know what she's gonna do. So don't mess with 'er. You can't fool Mother Nature, but she sure can fool you! And will!"

Harry paused to be sure they took his meaning. "You kids go get your radios and head home while she'll still let ya. You just forget that party now, ya hear?"

"Aww, Harry," Ivan whined.

September looked out the small porthole glowing amber. "It is a beautiful morning," she said, somehow feeling none of his urgency over the weather. "But we'll go."

"Yes ya will. Many a sailor's last day began with a beautiful mornin', Little Miss." The television blinked to life, and Harry turned his attention to its cold electric light.

"Go home now," he said.

◆ ◆ ◆

Amid the screeching gulls, groaning boat hoists, and cursing deck hands attending to their Saturday-morning duties, Ivan and September carted their packs along the dock. The sun finally broke over the icy mountain peaks standing beyond the little town. With it came heat and hope.

It was their first time alone together since September's conversation with their father, and she was waiting to hear what Ivan thought of the whole thing. They were nearly to the skiff before he spoke.

"What's Dad going to say when he hears the real story?"

"I'll try to straighten the whole thing out tonight." September slipped the pack from her shoulder and let it down into the *Four-O-Five*. "I tried to tell him the truth. You heard me. Once he knows we're home safe and the radios are fixed, maybe he'll let us stay at the cove."

Ivan slumped his pack on top of his sister's. "Why would he?"

"Well, because…" September stepped from the shadow of the harbor master's shack into the warm sunlight. "Because that's where he thought we were last night and it was okay then. He trusts us out there. You heard him say it."

"He said it because he had no idea we broke every single deal we made," Ivan scoffed. "Do you really think he'll trust us after today?"

"Yes." September started walking to the ramp, then stopped. "I mean, I think so. I mean, I don't know anymore, Ivan! We did our work, we had the radios repaired with our own money, and we tricked ol' Mooseburger out of contacting the authorities. Dad is always telling us to be responsible, and we were, weren't we?"

"I guess we were," Ivan agreed with what he wanted to hear. "We haven't goofed up anything since my megagoof with the radios."

"So do we go turn ourselves in to Aunt Nelda right when everything is back to normal?" September started up the ramp again.

Ivan fell in behind her. "No way. And he did tell us to be home by the radio today."

"That's right," September said, relaxing with their decision. "I wonder what his big surprise is?"

Ivan made a sour face. "Probably a new chain saw, or a Rototiller, or a meat grinder. You know how his surprises are no surprise."

Ivan froze. He had totally forgotten. "Ground meat! Sep, what about ol' Mooseburger? What's he gonna do when we go back without Dad?"

"Dad was sick, remember?" September said offhandedly. "We'll tell Berger he stayed in town to see the doc and sent us back home to work. By the time Berger figures out we fooled him, he won't have time to do anything about it before Dad really does come home."

"Boy, you've really got this figured, don't you?" Ivan walked along beside his sister, taking her measure.

"Everything will work out," she promised.

Ivan cast a backward look at the Dockside Traders and decided to take the real measure of September's confidence. "So, can we stop by the party for a while?"

Feeling like her compass of right and wrong was badly out of adjustment, September took a few steps before answering. "I'd like to, but we can't. Harry's right. We should head straight home."

Ivan detected weakness. "Harry's not the boss of us!" he declared.

"Forget it," she said, stronger now.

"It's *free videos*, Sep." As soon as he said it, Ivan knew he'd taken the wrong tack.

"Ivan Crane, you make me crazy!" September opened her arms at the top of the ramp as if to summon the higher power of the whole beautiful morning. "It's a fine day in September. Tonight we'll sleep in our own beds listening to the loons call instead of listening to loony Uncle Spitz snoring at Aunt Nelda's, and still all you can think about is *video games!*" She closed her hands around Ivan's neck and pretended to strangle him. "Snap out of it!"

"Okay, okay, I was just asking." Ivan pushed her arms away and kicked some dirt ahead of himself as they made their way down the road. "Let's go get the stupid radios."

September checked her watch. "It's just ten now, so they're open."

They turned the corner to the electronics shop and walked squinting into the bright sun all the way there.

"The parts didn't come in until late yesterday," the technician said from his workbench. He looked at Ivan over the top of his eyeglasses. "I need another hour on these—you burned up both power supplies, you know."

"I know," Ivan said meekly, feeling like a criminal as he turned to leave. "See you in an hour."

"Totally burned out and ruined, and I don't know what you thought you were—" Ivan heard the man complaining until the door closed behind him.

September was sitting against the front of the building with her wool coat opened and her face tipped toward the sun. Ivan joined her.

"Another hour, Sep," he said, twisting his rubber boot heels into the dry dirt road.

"Mmm," September moaned contentedly with her eyes closed. "I think I'll spend it right here."

A shadow passed in front of the sun and spoke to them. "Aren't you guys going to TC's party?"

Startled, Ivan and September looked up to see Sheri and Annette standing over them. Sheri had a wrapped gift in her hands. She wore improbably white running shoes September thought had to be right out of the box, creased jeans, and a dainty sweater. Annette was dressed much the same, only cleaner, if that was possible.

September drew her big boots in from the dirt and closed her coat. "Hi, Sheri. Hi, Annette."

"C'mon, it's an early party and we're late! Free games, free hot dogs, and *Dockside* fries!"

Sheri offered a hand and pulled September to her feet alongside Ivan, who stood eagerly brushing the dust off the seat of his pants.

"We can't go to the party," September said, embarrassed.

"Why not?" Ivan, Sheri, and Annette asked at once.

"We look like…like bush rats!" September looked down helplessly at the clothes she'd slept in, then remembered the real issue when she looked at her brother. "Besides, we have to go home, Ivan."

"Not for an hour!" Ivan said desperately. "We can't go without the radios!"

"You look fine—come for an hour!" Sheri said.

"You have to meet TC's mom—she's so nice. She invited us personally," Annette boasted.

"One hour!" Ivan pleaded.

September allowed herself to be led from the wall with Sheri and Annette on either side. There was no point in not going, she thought. They had to wait somewhere.

"Okay, but only for an hour," she agreed, smoothing her rumpled boat clothes as best she could.

CHAPTER 14

When they went through the front door of the Dockside, a wave of sound and scent met them. Sweet cocoa smells mixed with the everyday odor of the Dockside fryer. The chatter and laughter of twenty kids poured from the game room. The sulking cook at the fryer leaned over a puff of greasy steam.

"You're here!" TC called from clear across the snack shop. He rose from a table buried under gifts and envelopes. A colorful cake dominated another table. A woman was putting the final artistic touches on the cake design with a tiny tube of icing. "Hi, Sheri. Hi, Annette. Ivan! September! You made it! Come meet my mom!"

Sheri and Annette moved to where TC's mom stood waiting with a welcoming smile. Sheri put her gift on the table with the others and said hello.

"Nice to see you again, Sheri. Hello, Annette."

"Hello, Ms. Barron." Both girls smiled brightly. The woman turned to Ivan and September, who still stood fidgeting a distance away. She strode toward them and opened both arms.

"And you must be the Ivan and September I've heard so much about. How do you do? I'm Gabrielle Barron."

September smiled as brightly as the other girls had. TC's mom took September's hand in both of hers and said, "I'm so pleased to meet you."

September could not look away from the woman's face. A face that seemed wholly focused on her. "Nice to meet you too, Ms. Barron."

"Please call me Gabrielle," she said, and held September's hand a warm moment longer.

Then she respectfully turned to Ivan, who was staring at the games blazing away in the other room.

"I'm so happy you could come to TC's party, Ivan," she said.

"We can't stay long," Ivan blurted, only looking at her for as long as it took to say it.

"I'm sorry to hear that." Gabrielle chuckled, amused at Ivan's impatience with the formalities. "TC, why don't you and Ivan play some games while I show September to the hot chocolate."

"Thank you, ma'am," Ivan gushed.

"Thanks, Mom! See ya later!"

Gabrielle and September shared an easy laugh as the boys vanished into the commotion of the game arcade. They walked together to the table where Sheri and Annette still stood admiring the cake and arranging the gifts. September felt a twinge of shame.

"We didn't think we were coming and don't have a gift," she confided.

Gabrielle put an arm softly around September's shoulders. "Don't you worry about that for one minute. TC's just happy you're here. He's spoken of nothing but you and your brother for the past two days."

"Really?" September grinned and gave in to the soft squeeze on her arm before Gabrielle released her.

"Yes, I think you've become his Alaskan heroes. All he knows is the city, and he can't believe how you live out there. I must confess I'm quite impressed myself. He talks about your cabin across the bay constantly. And your boat and pet bear."

September laughed. "He's hardly a pet!"

Gabrielle poured a steaming mug of cocoa from a thermos and handed it to September. "TC has a big imagination. I'm sure there's a lot that he's misunderstood about your interesting lives. It's so different from what we knew in Seattle."

September sipped at her cocoa while Gabrielle glanced at the game room and then leaned closer. "TC is such a city boy, but he's always loved nature and the great outdoors. Now, being surrounded by it like this, well—I think it nearly overpowers him sometimes."

September felt at home in Gabrielle's warm confidence. "It overpowers a lot of us," she said.

"He said you were having some trouble with your radios. Is that true?"

"Yes," September said. "But they're being fixed. At eleven we have to get them and go back across the bay in case the weather turns bad. That's why we can't stay."

The expression on Gabrielle Barron's soft face was a mixture of messages—all good ones.

"Such exciting lives!" the woman declared, looking at September in gracious amazement before including Sheri and Annette in her attentions.

"So, how would you all like to help me finish with these decorations before lunch?"

She tossed each of them a roll of crepe paper, and laughing easily together, they attacked the snack bar with tape and paper twists of bright color.

September didn't notice the time until she stuck one end of a streamer to the wall clock with a wad of masking tape.

"Eek! It's already eleven-fifteen?"

Reluctantly she made her way through the crowd of kids huddled around their flashing game consoles to find her brother. Ivan was thrashing on the buttons of one particularly noisy game at the center of a very large bundle of boys. She spotted TC on the edges and joined him.

"Your mom is so great, TC."

"Yeah. She's pretty cool." TC grinned without taking his eyes from whatever it was Ivan was accomplishing on the frantic display before them. "Your brother can really rock on Tech Patrol. Look at that score!"

September saw a number so long she would not have known what to call it.

"Impressive," she said, guessing it was. "But we gotta go."

"Not yet!" Ivan yelled over the din without so much as glancing from his battle plan. "I can break the record!"

Video poisoning, September thought, and looked out the window facing the bay. A slight breeze wrinkled the water just enough to catch the sun and scatter it like diamond dust.

"Well, I don't see any problems out there. I'll get the radios and put them on the boat. But when I get back, we go. Deal?"

Ivan grunted as he flamed something else on-screen.

"Deal," he said. "Thanks, Sep."

She walked back through the snack shop, where TC's mom was distributing platters piled high with hot dogs and sizzling French fries.

"Will you at least come back for lunch and cake?" Gabrielle asked. "It's such a lovely day."

September smiled somewhat reluctantly, then snatched two hot fries from the passing tray. She felt her willpower disappear along with the fries and her reluctance soon followed. "Of course. I wouldn't miss it."

She swept through the door licking her fingers and set out down the sunny street. What harm is a little cake on a lovely day? she thought, and noticed her reflection in the passing windows—a hurried girl in canvas and rubber with her hair trailing in the breeze behind her.

"September Crane, Alaskan hero!" she declared, laughing to her window double.

September balanced the slippery plastic-wrapped radios on the railing at the top of the ramp. A cool whiff of wind scrambled her long hair over her face, and she noticed the harbor flags flapping sleepily across the way.

The *Williwaw* sat in its slip. "Har har har!"

Ahh, good ol' Big and Hairy, she thought. You always know where he is on a Saturday morning.

Bearing her load down to the *Four-O-Five*, she jumped into the boat and considered the safest place to transport the delicate radios. They had been wrapped water-tight by the technician, but needed to be cushioned. Their backpacks were already bulging, so she pulled aside the rain gear covering the dummy dad. Unzipping the front of the coverall, she dug a cavity in the loose chips and sawdust and gently nestled the radios inside. She closed the zipper again and checked around.

Everything appeared to be as they had left it. She hefted the full gas tank and then the other. Deciding it was low—maybe just enough to get them home—she resolved to fill it before they left. Their dad didn't like to have an empty tank on board.

Your extra gas can should stay like that—extra!

"Yes, Dad," she said playfully, replacing the rain gear over the dummy and heading for the ramp. A cool gust caught her by surprise at the top of the incline, and she stopped for a moment to close her jacket. As she did she heard a grind and a whir and then a familiar cough. She turned and saw oily black smoke erupt from the stack of the *Williwaw* as the dependable old diesel motor fired up, hesitated, then settled into the *blump-blump-blump* of Harry's warm-up idle.

Fearing she'd be spotted if Harry was in his pilothouse, September bolted down the rough town road toward the Dockside. She ran fast and hard and never looked back once. Not to see the dust she raised, nor the wind that followed, nor the gray pack of clouds growling up behind the mountain peaks and spilling over the glaciers down toward the long, wavy valleys leading into Bag Bay.

◆◆◆

"September! You're just in time! Come sit over here." Gabrielle Barron waved her in from the door.

TC sat beside his mother already well into his gifts and clowning with a half-eaten hot dog. September took the empty chair between Gabrielle and Ivan.

"TC sure makes friends easily," September remarked, helping herself to one of Ivan's fries.

"We thought this party would be a good way to introduce ourselves to all of you," his mom said. "But I think he'd already met everybody on Bag Bay. TC has a gift for gab!"

September smiled. "I noticed."

"Who's ready for carrot cake?" Gabrielle asked the group.

While TC and his mom dished out cake, September and Ivan helped pass it around. September relished the job. She met more kids in ten minutes than she'd met in the last ten years. Each table had a ring of friendly faces. *Hello, I'm Norman. Thank you, I'm Laura. What's your name? I'm Angela. Can I have the piece with the flower?*

No one looked at her boots. No one said anything about her dumpy coat or the way her hair splayed down off her head. She was TC's friend. That's all they knew, and that's all they needed. September hadn't been to a lot of parties, but she was positive this was going to be the one to beat for the rest of her life.

As the other guests devoured birthday cake in preparation for the next round in the game room, she ate hers slowly, enjoying the moment. "Isn't this wonderful, Ivan?"

Ivan plunged his fork into another bite. "I would've rather had chocolate."

"I mean the party!"

149

"Sure," Ivan conceded. "If I could only break the record on Tech Patrol."

September couldn't stand it. "Is that all you came for?"

Ivan looked at her as if she were made of wood. "Of course! Can we stay a little while longer? Please?"

"You are hopeless." September regarded the clear blue bay out the window and nodded her okay.

"Hopeless, maybe. Helpless, never!" Ivan clutched his hands in front of him in gaming position. "Hey, TC. Ready for round two?"

TC shoveled the last of his cake into his face and talked around it. "You're on, bush rat!"

A general migration of video heads followed the two boys back to the game room, leaving September and Gabrielle alone at the table. Gabrielle was looking out at the bay with a far-off smile.

"What a beautiful place this is," she said.

"Yes," September agreed, looking too.

The *Williwaw* swept into view beyond the harbor wall. "Oh, look, Gabrielle! That's Harry and our mail boat!"

The two watched the boat chugging out into the bay. A low roll and trailing wind slapped against its stern and sent little plumes of silver spray into the sunlight. The water was jade green with caps of shining white foam. A man in orange rain gear stood in the bow of the boat looking across the bay. September could barely see Harry's outline in the wheelhouse.

"Are they going to your cabin?" Gabrielle asked.

"No, not today." September thought for a moment. "It's

probably some stray tourist looking for eagles or whales or something. Harry does that on his days off."

"Sounds wonderful." Gabrielle studied the scene for a while longer and then said, "It looks rather choppy out there. Aren't you worried about getting home? I've heard this water is so very cold and dangerous!"

September glanced out the window and assumed an air of bravado. "Actually, this bay can kill you from hypothermia in less than half an hour if you're unlucky enough to go in it."

Gabrielle gave her an astonished look, to September's great delight.

"The trick," she went on, "is to stay out of the water."

Again she looked nonchalantly out at the bay. "This is nothing. Just our regular day breeze. It will push us all the way home like a ride on a slide!"

"Very poetic!" said Gabrielle, laughing.

"Besides," September continued, "Harry doesn't like bad weather, and he wouldn't be out with tourists if he thought it was going to storm."

"Then I won't worry."

Gabrielle patted September twice on the arm and rose to begin picking up platters and plates. September did the same, and some other kids helped as well. They wiped down the smeared tables, grabbing up battered paper plates, not saying very much at all.

After clearing the front corner table, September stopped and looked out again at the *Williwaw*. She could still see it far out in the bay. The white paint of the wheelhouse was all that signaled its location as it flashed in the sun on an occasional lucky roll.

Never wave a ship out of sight. September thought of her dad's superstitions and looked away from the boat. As she did, the world outside seemed to shift.

She looked again, and to her horrid amazement a sick yellow and gray shadow drew slowly across the harbor and out into the bay. She felt a cold fear climbing her backbone. Leaning forward, she gazed up in time to see the sun disappear behind a bank of roiling black clouds coming hard and fast from nowhere.

"Ivan!" she screamed just once. Her brother appeared wide-eyed in the arcade doorway nearly before the loose plates from September's hand had hit the floor.

Ivan saw the blue day pale and the bright green sea turn cement-colored from where he stood. "Oh, no!"

September held the door while Ivan fumbled around for his coat. TC came out and stood by his mom. Annette and Sheri were by the trash can looking slightly unhinged by September's sudden outburst.

"Tell everyone good-bye for us." September tried to appear poised. "It was a wonderful party, Gabrielle. I was so pleased to meet you."

It sounded goofy and she knew it, but it was the best she could do under the circumstances. Ivan dashed through the door under her arm. September looked at TC and his mom and forced a brave smile.

"Don't worry!" she yelled, letting go of the jangling door.

"We do this all the time!" And Ivan ate her dust all the way to the harbor.

CHAPTER 15

September stalled at the bottom of the ramp and faced the bleak weather front closing down on the bay like the lid on a giant pressure pot. When Ivan caught up to her he said, "I don't like this, Sep. It's moving too fast."

"It's fine!" she puffed desperately, needing it to be. "I saw Harry leave just half an hour ago!" Grabbing her brother's hand, she pulled him around the side of the harbor shack. "Harry had a tourist with him, and he would never go out if it was a real storm. If we hurry it'll be a good tailwind, that's all."

Ivan looked up at the port flags, which whipped and quivered against the gathering gray sky. "That's quite a tailwind."

"A following sea!" September argued, stepping into the *Four-O-Five*. "The 'north wind blows you all the way home,' remember? We'll be there in no time!"

Ivan folded his arms against the wind and the idea and made no move toward the boat. "I think we should wait it out."

"Where?"

"We could go back to the party, and if it doesn't calm down before it's over we'll have TC's mom drive us out to Aunt Nelda's."

Ivan sounded practical—too practical. September suspected something else. "You just want to get back to your stupid video games!" she shouted. "Even if it means being stranded at the homestead!"

The part of it that was true made Ivan's temper flare. "And *you* can't admit you blew it! You just couldn't tear yourself away from *Gabrielle Fancy Pants*!"

The part of this that was true triggered September to whip Ivan's rain gear into his face and scream, "Watch what you say, *Little Mister*!"

"Stop calling me that!" Ivan threw the gear back at his sister. He might have jumped in the boat right after them had the harbor master not come around the corner.

"So it's you makin' all this racket out here!" The man searched with his whole head to find them in his walleyed gaze. "You're that Steamer Cove bunch agin, eh?"

"Yes, sir," Ivan said stiffly, feeling caught.

The man rubbed the hide of one hand against his stubbled chin and snorted with amusement. "I jus' seen your ol' man a while ago!"

September doubted it. "You saw our dad?"

"Just now. Harry was takin' him across on the *Williwaw*. Some sorta surprise!" He paused to gather his wind. "Hoo-hoo! Surprise! He's over there, and you're over here!"

The news barreled through September like ice water. Dad knew he was coming home early the whole time, she thought. Of course. That's why he was so sweet last night. He wasn't even calling from Dutch Harbor. He was probably already in Anchorage. He wanted them around the cabin and not off clamming or doing something in the woods when he got there! That was his surprise!

"He'll go berserk if we're not there!" Ivan had figured it out, too, and was already climbing into the boat after his rain gear.

"We gotta catch up with them!" September knew Harry could not have seen the *Four-O-Five* still tied behind the building. For all he knew they'd left hours ago. What would they think?

"They'll think we sank!" Ivan finished her thought.

The old man continued cackling, until he worked himself into a thick and bottomless cough. He pulled a rag from his pocket and held it to his face while September begged him.

"You have to try to reach the *Williwaw* on the radio and tell them we're on our way!" September waited to see if he understood. His eyes were wet with laughter, and his face bobbed up and down with every convulsive hack.

"Do you understand?"

The head continued to bob.

"Go. Go! Tell them we're coming!" September pulled the starter cord so hard she nearly went over when it roared up and set at an urgent idle. While she wriggled into her life jacket and Ivan connected the last straps on his, they watched the harbor master weave his way down the side of the building. His whole body dipped and rose in agreement with every spasm until he disappeared around the corner.

A gust of wind wormed its way under the ramp and flipped September's hood up behind her head as if recommending it. She tied the strings tight below her chin while Ivan cleared the lines and poled them away from the float with an oar.

"Let's get ready for some rock 'n' roll," he said, more to himself than to his sister as he stumbled through the tangle of lines and clam buckets that littered the length of the skiff.

September swung them into the main channel to the harbor entrance and watched as Ivan sorted things out. He secured the oars to the seats with some line so they couldn't be lost overboard. There were two sturdy white bailing buckets and a length of good towing line. September asked him to move them to where they were close at hand. He stepped on the dummy lying between the seats and she barked at him to be careful of the radios. He moved the dummy to the front of the boat with the two packs to help balance the weight. September nodded in approval, knowing if the stern was too heavy in a big following sea, the *Four-O-Five* might swamp.

The toolbox sat between September's feet, and she opened it to check the flare pistol. Ivan noticed and turned a wary eye to the blackening bay.

"How bad you think it is out there?" He sat on the middle seat and watched as September folded open the gun, checked the load, and closed it again.

"Not that bad," she said, reassuring herself.

Ivan gripped the seat and set his jaw. September put the gun back into the dry toolbox and studied her brother's worried face.

"I watched Harry leaving and it looked fine, just a steady push like the other night," she said. "Besides, they'll turn around to meet us once they know we're coming."

Ivan said nothing and looked over her shoulder toward the harbor office, imagining the old man coughing into a microphone.

"Maybe we should wait for them," he said, and then noticed movement in the street above. TC and a few others were standing near the Dockside seeing them off. "Look!"

September turned, and she brightened at the sight, waving big and long like her brother while guiding them around the breakwater. The wind grabbed at her loose sleeves and whispered around the openings of her hood.

"See you later!" she yelled, as if they could hear.

Idling along in the calm waters downwind of the wall, they saw a sea otter holding her pup tight to her belly and back-paddling straight for the skiff. September arced their course around the peaceful critters, who kept four black eyes fixed on them the whole way by.

Ivan watched the pair go. "I said why don't we wait for Dad and Harry to come back for us?"

September looked out at the humped gray backs of the waves moving ahead of her leading directly to Steamer Cove and home. "What if the harbor master didn't get through?" she said with a blast of guilt. She pictured her father's terrified face as he entered the empty cove. The skiff gone. The cabin all closed up. "Dad will think we drowned," she insisted.

"Dad's going to kill us anyway," Ivan said gravely. "You know Harry's told him what we've been up to all week."

"Ivan, I *have* to explain what happened!" September added speed as they slipped out from behind the wall. "C'mon, we're only half an hour behind them!"

Ivan held on to his seat as the first swell nudged them onward, and September goosed the throttle to keep up with it.

"A half hour to live," he said, grimly watching the next dark swell rise up around Point Thumb and topple toward them in the wind.

Once they caught up with the wind and waves, Ivan had to admit the sea wasn't nearly as scary as the prospect of facing their father. September was able to keep the *Four-O-Five* pitched forward on the face of a roller so that their speed matched that of the swells. The wind at their tail felt tame now that they were keeping some pace with it. Ivan moved next to September. Both kids tried to find some comfort in their favorite sport of skiff surfing. The forward half of the boat was totally out of the water as they skimmed effortlessly along with the aft end firmly in the grip of the rolling sea.

"Wow! We *are* flying!" he shouted.

"Harry can't do this on that big tub of his!" September exclaimed.

That was true, thought Ivan. Both of them held a vision of catching up with the *Williwaw*. Sweeping up behind the poky mail boat hooting and hollering. Their dad, mad or not, waving from the front deck as they circled around and raced him home.

"Woo-hoo!" they cried as the wave they'd hitched a ride on seemed to leap ahead in the wilder winds away from shore.

Ivan looked back over the foaming crest and caught a glimpse of the town falling far behind them. "We'll be halfway before you know it!"

Halfway across Bag Bay was the worst place to be, September thought. She wanted to be all the way across. The roaring motor had just one squeeze of throttle left to offer, and September twisted her whole arm to get the last of it, chanting as she did.

"The north wind blows you all the way home!"

"To me!" Ivan finished with their mother's words. The cold realization of where their mother was and how she got there slid with them down into the slippery trough. They watched in dismay as the pointed bow knifed into the back of the wave ahead.

It was like running into a gigantic Jell-O mold. Ivan and September lurched forward as the *Four-O-Five* swallowed a gulp of green water over the bow before being spit back into the face of the following wave.

"Whoops!" September pulled herself up and regained control of the tiller, commanding, "Bail, Ivan!"

Ivan was already crouched and dragging a bucket through shin-deep water and over the side. "I'm on it!" he called, deftly scooping seawater while he rode the bucking skiff.

With the pause in their momentum, the sea charged under them like stampeding buffaloes. Each wave launched the *Four-O-Five* up and over its back and directly into the path of the next. The dummy with the radios flew into the air spewing stuffing. Ivan watched it flailing around, loose-limbed like a person having a seizure, until it landed on the rail half out of the boat and began to slither into the bay.

"The radios!"

Ivan lunged for the dummy and wrestled it back into the bottom of the flooded skiff. September gunned the throttle with both hands and aimed them back in cadence with the ranks of gray swells.

"We're too heavy, Ivan! You have to bail some more!"

Ivan heaved the dummy aside. The wind continued to drive the ever-steeper waves at them. Meaner gusts tore off the frothing wave tops and splattered them into the boat.

Blinking the stinging salt spray from his eyes, Ivan braced himself between seats and scooped out the unwelcome seawater like a determined machine.

The *Four-O-Five* struggled up the long sloped back of a wave and crested over the top.

"It's working!" September cried, immediately cutting back on the throttle so as not to repeat her mistake and plunge too quickly into the hollow ahead. At the bottom of the trough the swell behind would lift them and pass smoothly underneath as September powered forward and up the back again.

Ivan captured the last of what water he could with the awkward bucket and then plopped next to his sister at the tiller. "This is worse than we thought. Shouldn't we go back?"

"We can't! We'll never make any headway going against this! Don't worry, we'll make it as long as we keep going!"

Ivan looked back. All he saw was a wall of water shimmering like black silk. September pegged the motor, and they shot up the face so fast he felt his insides compact. From the crest he saw the town far beyond the angry white tops of the waves lined up behind them like an advancing army. His guts floated into his throat as the skiff fell into the next trough.

She's right, he thought, swallowing hard. We'd never make enough progress going against this blow to reach town again. We'd be lucky to hold our own against it. There's only one way home and no turning back. He shuddered inside his rain gear, soaking wet to his soul.

September's bare hand gripped the tiller and grew steadily numb. She guided them through the sea as though it were an obstacle course, angling and timing her attacks with the imperfect rhythm of the bay. She surged forward and back as the *Four-O-Five* climbed, then coasted, climbed and coasted—the groaning motor complaining like a muck-mired cow.

We're doing fine, but this is going to use up a lot of gas, September thought. *Gas!* Oh no, we forgot to top off the tank!

She reached for the tank they were using and felt a lance of terror as it lifted without resistance. She shook it and felt nothing. "Ivan! We have to change tanks!"

Ivan immediately understood the alarm in her voice. If they let the gas line run dry, they'd be faced with priming and restarting the barren engine while at the mercy of the chaos thrashing around them. Without power they could not steer, and the long skiff would naturally turn sideways to the sea. They would not be long in this world after that.

"You keep us steady!" he said, turning to the task.

Ivan blew hot breath on his sluggish fingers. The fuel line simply clipped from one tank to the other, and the motor would continue to run between tanks on what little fuel was left in the line.

He shook life into his hands and plucked the gas line from the first tank. A tongue of wind-driven foam licked over the side and smacked his eyes. He wiped at them with an unfriendly rubber sleeve while clutching the open gas line. September looked intently ahead, continuing to work them through the treacherous sea.

When Ivan's eyes cleared, he saw coming right behind them a massive, frothing evil thing—a wave easily twice the size of the others. It welled up so dark and high and startling that a pitiful clucking noise escaped his throat and warned September. She looked just in time to see that they could never take such a wave over their stern without swamping. She pushed the tiller hard over, gunned the engine, and turned their bow to it.

The top of the monster collapsed and cascaded across the skiff as they burst through the other side now facing into the siege. The next wave, though smaller, took advantage of everything in the flooded skiff being afloat and untethered. As it pitched their bow skyward and then abruptly dropped them again, the gas cans lurched over the side and bobbed loose in the turmoil red as fresh wounds. Right behind them went the two packs, one after the other.

Ivan still clung to the loose fuel line and lunged for the nearer of the escaped tanks. Half out of the boat himself and sightless in the salt-laced wind, he felt his palm brush the metal can and his fingers closed over the handle. It felt full.

"Got it!" he screamed.

September grabbed at a flap of her brother's raincoat and helped haul him back aboard. Ivan struggled to lift the heavy can, then found the strength at the sound of the faltering engine. The motor sputtered once while a desperate September nursed the throttle.

"Hurry!"

Ivan forced the can down between his knees in the wildly heaving water they'd taken on. Pinning it to the boat bottom in the violent pounding, he found the connection and jammed it into place.

"Go!" he yelled, and leaped to the bailing bucket without hesitation.

September feverishly pumped the primer bulb. She heard the motor gain strength and even out. She held them steady into the sea, fearful of exposing their stern to the ever-building gale. The packs had vanished, and the other bucket was missing. She looked ahead to what lay in their wicked future and could see no farther than the next wave.

Now that they were facing the exact opposite direction than they wanted to go, the punishment seemed doubled. It was the same nightmare in reverse. She motored up the faces of the relentless waves and cut the throttle as soon as they broke over the tops. Then they crashed down into the boiling gully with such force the boat's wooden planking would squeak.

The sea's assault was so rapid that even as they labored mightily into it, the *Four-O-Five* was being driven backward. All they were accomplishing was staying afloat and surviving each wave as it hammered them around Bag Bay.

Ivan gasped for breath, his arms almost too spent to lift the bucket to the rail. He had bailed the greater share of water over and used what strength he had left to redistribute the load. He grabbed the dummy by a leg and hauled it with the hard-won radios to the stern. He used the plunging motion of the boat to help lift the toolbox over a seat and back.

"We need to keep the bow up!" he said, collapsing onto

the aft seat beside September and squinting into the punishment coming their way.

September's face was set like stone. I have to keep it together, she instructed herself. A wave hit hard, jerking the tiller from her hand and knocking her to the side. Ivan snatched her sleeve and helped her hand find the way back to its station.

September leaned her weight toward him to steady herself and felt him lean back. "We won't make it this way, Ivan! We can't go back, and I don't dare turn toward home again. We could never take this from behind!"

September started quaking, and Ivan couldn't tell his tears from seawater. He peered down at the dummy holding the radios. "Why did I ever mess with these stupid things," he cursed at the bundle.

"I'm so sorry, Sep," he said, and bent to the toolbox. Pulling out the flare pistol, he turned to his sister.

"It's my fault," she said. "Do it."

Ivan braced himself, waited to crest the next wave, then raised the gun with both hands. "I hope somebody's watching!" he said, and squeezed the trigger. A red-hot signal flare erupted like a jet-powered pixie into the gigantic grayness surrounding them. It streaked upward in an ever-sagging trajectory and hung for two blinks before being snuffed in the hungry waters of Bag Bay.

"Do another!" September cried, spitting froth from the last crusher.

Ivan broke open the pistol, ejected the spent cartridge, and groped in the toolbox for a second flare. A surging roller knocked the boat hard. The box tipped and scattered the cartridges in a confusion of screwdrivers, pliers, and knives. I have to get a flare up higher and for longer than the last one if Dad, if *anyone*, is going to spot it and come to our aid, he thought. He finally captured a new load and jammed it in with nearly useless fingers. One more chance, he thought, and hoped if he fired it up and into the wind it might get more hang time.

Ivan braced his legs against the seat ahead and readied the pistol to fire as they came over the top of another steep swell. When they broke through the biting spray he opened his eyes to shoot and was met with a paralyzing spectacle.

September shrieked at the appalling size of the wave ahead.

The sinister rogue stood before them as if it had been lurking there all the while, waiting to pounce. The skiff plummeted into the hole in the ocean at the foot of the fiend. The seething mass of frigid water loomed before Ivan and September and roared above the feeble groan of the motor trying to push them over and free of it.

"Forget the flare!" September screamed. "Hold on to something!"

CHAPTER 16

The *Four-O-Five* responded and lifted its nose, at last, up the steely wet slope. Ivan fired the flare pistol. The burning red hope flashed to life and died with a sudden sizzling gasp as it disappeared into the belly of the rogue.

The crest of the giant toppled over onto them in an icy waterfall. Ivan found himself washed from his seat and separated from the boat as the ocean tore at him. He let go of the flare gun and thrashed around for a handhold. He felt as if he were swimming and falling and flying at once. His hand brushed something and he snatched at it—another hand. Ivan and September poured from the back of the wave and sprawled arm in arm across the middle of their nearly swamped skiff.

"You okay?" she sputtered.

As the unattended motor idled aimlessly, the skiff floated crosswise in the waves, and Ivan grabbed the railing to brace for the next onslaught. They tipped dangerously to one side but recovered, to their relief, with most of the green water spilled from the boat. "I'm okay! Can you steer?" he asked.

September crabbed her way to the tiller while Ivan strained

once again to the bailing. The bow swung back into the sea with a roar of the motor, followed by a chattering sound and a death rattle. They both looked to where the gas tank should have been. It wasn't anymore. The fuel line was broken off at the motor housing. The engine coughed like the harbor master and quit. The *Four-O-Five* languished now in the throes of the storm, helpless as a log.

The low throaty howl of the wind sounded all the louder in the quiet that blared from the dead engine. The waves smacked the crippled skiff before loping off toward Steamer Cove. September still held the useless tiller, momentarily lost for any solutions. The skiff swung sideways into the trough, pitching like a canoe.

Caught open in the wind, the empty toolbox flipped into the sea and cartwheeled out of sight. Ivan scrambled through the skiff, madly searching for the flare gun, tossing aside tools and tackle. Gone! he screamed inside. The boat stood on its railing and hesitated there for a long horrible moment while Ivan clung to the oarlock.

"Sep! We'll turn over!"

Ivan grappled with one of the stowed oars. We *have* to get our bow turned back into the waves, he thought. He got the oar over the side and into the oarlock, then reached for the other. With fingers that ached like raw bone, he tore at the line securing the oar to the seat.

"Sep! Do something!" he hollered, snatching at a rusty bait knife lying in the shifting debris. He sawed at the strap just as they were savagely bucked sidelong.

The loose oar flung free of the skiff and twirled in the air as if it had been a marching baton. It plunged blade-first into the hammering swells, shot to the surface, and drifted off.

September had an idea. "We need a sea anchor!" she shouted as she jumped into action, hauling the towline and their last bucket to the bow.

"Good!" Ivan agreed, and continued hacking at the strap for the remaining oar.

September tied the line with a one-handed hitch to the bow ring as she clutched the cap rail with the other hand. Each broadside nearly capsized them. Just holding on took a brutal effort. Nothing lay between them and the frigid abyss below but luck and the hearty *Four-O-Five* that found its bottom time after terrifying time.

One more big wave would put them over in a whiff, though, and September worked desperately at her remedy. While fishing halibut last spring, her dad had taught her how to drag a bucket off the bowline when they drifted too fast in the wind. "Just enough to keep you turned into it," he'd said.

She secured the handle of the white bucket to the other end of the line and dropped the whole works over the side. It floated in a tangle. A steep wave nearly tossed it back into the skiff, and then the bucket slowly began moving away—spreading the line out behind it.

In the stern, Ivan had the freed oar wedged tight against the motor. He worked it like a rudder, pulling the stern to one side and pivoting the bow toward the sea.

"It's working!" September cried.

A wave quartered down their seaward side, coaxing them farther into the position they sought. The line to the sea anchor stretched tight, and the skiff fell back into a severe but predictable pounding. With the bow held into the wind by its shabby tether, the punishing bay rollers could toss but not turn them. Each wave pointed them up to the cloud-choked sky, then flopped them down into the bruising space between one menacing hump and the next.

Satisfied her drift anchor would hold them steady, September crawled back to where Ivan knelt exhausted by his efforts with the makeshift helm. Most of the beating was being taken by the bow, and there was a relative stability to the stern. She looked at her brother's ghostly face. So determined and so scared, she thought. "We're a good team," she said, wanting to see more of the determined.

Ivan's dulled and reddened eyes seemed to measure out the silent question, *Now what?*

"They'll come for us," she promised, taking her share of the oar and craning to see over the madness surrounding them.

How? Ivan thought, looking at the bay, now wind-whipped into such a lather of froth that it appeared to be a white bowl of cream. The wave faces careening at them were as black as portholes in a sunken ship. Ivan peered into each dark window, seeing pieces of his life washing by.

A month ago he was stuffing blueberries into his mouth while they all picked along the sunny ridge above Huckleberry Cove. September alongside filling her bucket and their father whistling a sweet sound in bushes ahead.

A week ago he was digging clams with his sister to keep from going to sorry old Aunt Nelda's. A day ago he was on his way to Aunt Nelda's anyway. An hour ago he was the hero of Tech Patrol, with dry feet, a belly full of cake, and two radios good as new. He let a weak smile move his blue lips.

"Know what, Sep?" Ivan paused to absorb a blast of spray.

"What?"

"Aunt Nelda's looks pretty good from here."

"Pigs and all," she agreed, and seized hold of the seat edge as the *Four-O-Five* dropped right out from under them.

They landed with a shriek of planking in the bottom of the trough. September crashed down onto the seat hard, but okay. Ivan had been caught completely by surprise and landed like a shot goose on top of the dummy. Ivan's face smacked on the seat, opening his forehead. Nobody had the oar.

A muddled Ivan sat up, holding on to nothing but his bleeding head as a wave levered the skiff into the air again. Like twin puppets, Ivan and the dummy were cast limply over the side. All that showed above the churning water was the orange ball of the dummy's head.

"Ivan!" September screamed as her brother's face appeared in the water, framed by the yellow collar of his life jacket. Sucking and spitting, his features were washed in pale red streaks of blood pouring from a cut the length of a finger on his forehead.

Moving as one piece up the front and down the back of every wave, the dummy now floated like a dead man between the boat and her brother. Ivan's panicked hands splashed around and found a sleeve of the coverall. September clamped one weakening hand on the center seat and cast herself half out of the *Four-O-Five*, coming up with the other sleeve in her fingertips.

She pressed her face and chest into the cap rail and summoned every fiber of might she had. The edge of the seat cut into her palm, and each surge threatened to pluck the dummy and her brother from her grasp.

"Hold on!" she shouted into the wood. The dummy stretched and tore but held.

A sound like a cracked whip followed by a hard slap across the arm turned her head to see that the anchor line had broken the bucket handle and recoiled into the skiff. With the sea anchor lost, the skiff swung back into the trough, and the dummy's arm went slack in her hands. The wind was pushing the boat hard and fast to where Ivan struggled in the numbing water.

September seized him by the strap of his life jacket. If he was pinned under the hull, the skiff would pound him to pieces. A swell vaulted the *Four-O-Five* onto its side like a dipper, and rather than being run over, Ivan poured in with the flood of water. His hands were still locked on to the dummy's sleeve. While September fought to pry loose Ivan's death grip, the boat tipped its rail again, and the dummy oozed over the side and rejoined them.

For a moment September lay in the tangle of line and brother and seawater—of wood chips, coverall, and radios—and she could have laughed. The urge was one of giving up, she knew. And she also knew that was the worst thought she could have. She'd heard the north country stories of hypothermia her whole life. People die from the cold when they stop trying and go to sleep.

"I gotta go," Ivan said right beside her.

She turned to face him. His eyes were open but not looking at anything. The cut bled freely down into his matted hair. He'd stopped shivering and looked oddly peaceful.

It's happening, she thought. Then, grabbing his shoulders, she demanded, "Ivan, snap out of it!"

"You snap out of it!" he snarled. "I'm going!"

"Where ya think you're going?" she asked, bracing against him as the boat tried to buck them over.

"TC's party," he declared, and made as if to stand up. "I can break the record."

"You can break your neck!" September pulled him down, and Ivan fought her with a burst of strength. She held tight.

"Let me go!" he cried, weakening, letting his head down.

"It's just the bump on your head, Ivan. And the cold." She pulled his hood back over his head and tried to speak calmly. "You're not going anywhere without me!"

They were only words, but she knew what to do as soon as she spoke them. Maybe the only thing she could do. Maybe the last thing she would do. Slipping quickly to the bow, she broke the line loose from the boat and brought the end back to where Ivan lay sloshing around with the dummy and the seawater.

"Ivan, listen to me!" she yelled, shaking terribly and gathering up the line strewn around the skiff. "We have to stay together!"

A brutal swell threw her down onto her brother and the dummy. She pulled the dummy's orange buoy into place between their chests as they lay crosswise in the bottom.

"This floats! It'll help!"

Ivan lay loose on the flooded bottom as September worked the line around his back and across her own. She looped it through the straps of their life jackets and cinched it tight.

"This is it—Little Mister!" She shuddered.

Ivan's eyes found hers just inches away from his face, and he focused through his thickening fog. "I told you not to call me that," he said.

September sucked short breaths through her convulsive tremors and listened to the storm gnashing at the *Four-O-Five* and howling over their heads in wicked rage. Each swell punched the skiff so far over on its rail that she and Ivan would be standing vertical to the world for a moment and then be pitched back the other way and drenched anew.

September had never felt so cold. The brief moments of calm when the boat stood them up with its bottom to the wind felt like warm spells, and in her own growing delirium she began to look forward to them.

Ivan started humming a tuneless melody with his eyes closed. September reached around the orange ball and worked her hands behind his shoulders, waiting. Her shivering eased, then quit as she rested her eyes and listened to him. Every time they swept upward she thought it would put them over. Then they would fall back, and the spray would lash their faces. There would be another—same thing—and down.

The rhythm of it settled her nerves in some absurd way, and she felt as if she too could drift off. It would be nice to sleep, she thought, just for a while. She began to recognize the tune Ivan hummed, and sang along with a thick tongue.

"The east wind blows you side to side."

The water shifting back and forth and back and forth.

"The west wind makes like a ride on a slide."

Up on their feet and down into the hollow again.

"A south wind mumbles warm and low."

Sweet sleep feels so warm.

"And the north wind blows you all the way home."

To me!

September opened her eyes again. Ivan's face was propped serenely against the orange ball tied between them. She pressed her cheek against the other side, looking out at the maelstrom.

"Home," she said. "I want to go home."

Ivan opened an eye and closed it.

"It's all my fault, Ivan." She spoke to the storm. "I stayed too long at the party and now it's all over."

"Game over," Ivan slurred.

September winced as a gust bit at her ears. She mocked herself in a bitter tone. "*It was so nice to meet you!* Now I must go kill my brother!"

Very poetic. The muffled voice of Gabrielle Barron echoed through September's cottony thoughts. *I won't worry.*

September let the cotton engulf her. A thin smile set across her face, and her tortured eyes grew calm, focusing far away.

"It's time to go home," she purred to the white fluffy wave tops.

Out of the many shades of relentless gray sweeping across her view, she witnessed a staggering flash of sharp black and brilliant white slip out of one wave and slide into the next.

Orcas, she thought happily...*Not killers*. Never killers.

Slowly, like the sun rising in a winter sky, it dawned anew on September that she was nowhere near her home. She was nowhere near anything. She was in the *Four-O-Five*. A skiff. A skiff in a storm—in peril.

"Ivan!" she shrieked. "Wake up!"

CHAPTER 17

September shook her brother. "We can't sleep!"

Ivan stirred and complained. "So tired…" he moaned.

"You've got to wake up and talk to me! We have to stay awake!" As she screamed, water hosed across Ivan's face, and his eyes opened wide. September seized the moment. "Tell me about…about Tech Patrol. What the heck *is* that game?"

"You don't care," Ivan murmured, trying to make his head comfortable against the dummy, smearing blood across the orange ball.

"I do," September insisted, shaking him some more. "How do you win?"

"You kill all the stupid vipers! How else?" he groaned.

Ivan sounded impatient. A good sign, thought September. "How do you kill them?"

"Blasters."

The rocking skiff kept the beat of their conversation.

Up.

"You blast them with blasters?"

Down.

"Of course you blast them with blasters! What else would you do with a blaster?"

Back.

"I don't know anything about blasters. How do they work?"

Forth.

"Sort of a cross between a plasma cannon and a photon torpedo."

Up.

Stuck for the next question, September paused, and in the pause she heard something on the wind.

Down.

Ivan needed no more prompting. "You see, a blaster fires at the speed of—"

"Shh!" September hissed, listening to the wind.

Back.

"I thought you wanted me to talk!"

Forth.

The *Four-O-Five* tipped to its rail, and in one great glimpse they saw the *Williwaw* breaking over the top of a wave. Their father was perched in the bow in orange rain gear, his hands cupped to his mouth.

"Dad!" Ivan and September wailed, waving their arms before rolling the other way again.

"I'm coming!" Mr. Crane brandished a boat hook on a long pole only two swells away.

The next time the skiff tipped, Ivan and September saw the *Williwaw* was upon them. A wave pounded their father to his knees. Harry's head ducked back into the pilothouse door, then out again as their dad regained his position.

"Back off, Harry!" he screamed over the wind and the roaring diesel as the two boats mashed each other. Ivan and September slid across the open skiff as it left a deep gouge down the side of the mail boat. "We'll crush them!"

Harry powered down, and the bigger boat fell back. Another wave crashed over their father. Then the diesel roared and their bow swung closer as Ivan and September tried to get off the bottom of the *Four-O-Five*. Tied together like Siamese twins with a buoy and a bag of wet sawdust sandwiched between them made it nearly impossible. Their dad poked the boat hook down into the skiff to snag the bowline, but September anxiously reached for it. Ivan rose with her, and their balance was lost as the skiff pitched under their feet.

They went over the side tied in a bundle of confusion, clutching each other and the curved end of the boat hook. They dangled from it for a long, hopeful moment before the next wave washed over them and their dad and wrenched the hook from their hands.

September swallowed the sea in gulps as their dad braced his chest against the railing that swooped over their heads and extended his arms helplessly to recover the dropped boat hook.

"I lost them!" he hollered, and pointed. "Don't run them down!"

"Dad," Ivan gurgled. September could hardly hear him.

"Hang on, Ivan." September tried to pull him higher on the orange ball between them, but it only made her head go under.

She kicked her booted feet uselessly in the paralyzing water, only managing to get them tangled up in the loose coverall. They bobbed around the convoluted ocean like corks. Their dad and the massive bottom hull of the *Williwaw* towered over them one moment, and then in the next, fell far below as Ivan and September were swept up the following swell. From the top September caught a glimpse of the *Four-O-Five* drifting away, still upright and bucking on the bay like a horse set free.

The water no longer felt cold. Ivan pulled his hood back, and September thought of bathtubs. The *Williwaw* disappeared into the next trough away from them. Ivan and September floated alone in their brief deep valley.

At the next crest she heard her father's command. "Bring them alongside!"

September could feel the powerful propeller of the *Williwaw* digging into the water as Harry poured on the throttle. The bow crashed through the wave separating them, and then the hulking mail boat lurched broadside to Ivan and September and idled down.

Blump-blump-blump. Harry's head popped out the door. "Make it count! I can't leave 'er crosswise like this!"

September hung limp in her life jacket as their dad scampered down the railing to midships and leaned down to snatch them. As he did, the next swell lifted the wad of her, Ivan, and the dummy high above their dad and the black deck below. They tumbled downward, and for a moment it appeared they'd be swept clear over the opposite side. The water pinned their father to the pilothouse and washed through the open door.

Ivan and September landed with a bone-bending thud on the wooden deck of the *Williwaw*—a boat christened for its captain's greatest fear. The wind moaned in the rigging and Harry's voice cut through the howling squall and spoke its name.

"Williwaw!" he bellowed. "Brace yourselves!"

The wall of wind crashed into them with the grinding force of a rock slide. Harry gunned the engine, trying to point his boat into the ambush. Sea spray raked the windows like bird shot.

The stout old boat staggered sideways, and its mast was driven down toward the wind-scalped waves. "We're going over!" Harry cried.

CHAPTER 18

Ivan and September tumbled across the pitched deck and slammed into the mast. Their dad clawed his way toward them as September tried desperately to cling to the slippery post. Unconscious, Ivan swung from their loop of rope with the dummy.

The boat continued rolling, and the deck tilted out from under them like a trapdoor back to the sea. September was pulled down the steep wet slope by Ivan's dead weight, and she couldn't hold on.

"Daddy!" she cried before jerking to a stop inches short of the railing.

"Got you!" her father shouted, clutching a cuff of the coverall and pawing his way along the loose leg like he would haul a fishnet. September felt the dummy dislodging from between her and Ivan. Ivan's limp figure started to slip from the loosened line, and she reached out and hooked his life vest in the crook of her arm.

"Hold us, Daddy!" she cried, reaching her other hand up to him.

"I won't let you go!" her father called through the chaos, and clasped her hand just as a torrent of water ripped across the boat.

The dummy tore away and was pulled down the deck head-first and lapped up by the surge—gone. The deck tipped straight up and down and the top of the mast reached for the sea.

"You can't have them!" their father screamed into the storm with one arm wrapped around the mast, the other hand on September, and his face stretched with pain and anger.

Gripped by her father above, gripping her brother below, September felt the fiber deep in her chest straining as if she would be torn in two pieces. She mustered every scrap of strength and will left in her.

September heard the engine growl far down in the heart of the faltering vessel, and she took power from it. She held her brother, her father held her, and somewhere through the terrible fray she knew Harry still had the helm and their fate in his hands. She felt the *Williwaw* beneath her heave against the williwaw surrounding her and slowly find its stubborn keel. The deck rose and gathered them up while the treachery of Bag Bay squirted from the scuppers and poured over the tail. The mast rose ponderously to the sky and caught the ragged coverall in the rigging, where it flapped overhead like a battle flag.

September gasped for breath as a defiant roar spilled from the shattered pilothouse windows above her. For one exquisite moment it drowned the sound of the wind and the water and the fear of it in her soul.

Har har har har harrrr! howled Harry. And the *Williwaw*,

shuddering under Ivan and September's spent bodies, turned once again to the sea.

Bong bong bong.

September's eyes floated open and closed. Ivan lay beside her on Harry's bunk, his face blank white, the gash in his forehead open and pink but not bleeding. She tried to say his name but only managed a muffled moan.

"You're okay, Temmy," she heard her dad say, and felt him jamming blankets around her and roughly rubbing her down head to foot. "We're going to get you home."

She looked around to find her dad and saw his shape move through the hatchway. The wavering light from outside showed their clothes and rain gear mixed with fragments of Harry's plates, cups, and television rushing forward and back in a mess of water and boiled cod. The big pot knocked against the table leg.

Bong bong bong.

Her eyes fluttered closed. Her body felt disconnected from her mind, as if it belonged to someone else. She shifted on the bunk, bumping into her brother with no more say in the matter than the table leg.

Dad's voice up the ladder.

"How's it look, Harry?"

Harry's voice sounded through the growling wind. "Still afloat. The storm blew 'erself out, an' she's settlin' some. Most of the bay is pumped back out of our hold, but we lost our antennas and can't call the harbor master or the Coast Guard to let 'em know we've survived. I hope they haven't come out lookin' for us. How's the kiddos?"

"Cold. Scary cold." Her dad was yelling in the cracked-open pilot-house. "I can't wake Ivan, and Temmy's sinking fast. Your stove went out when we took that water through the hatchway, and everything is trashed down below. We have to get 'em to the cabin."

"Don't ya worry. Long as we can sneak through those rocksa yers, we'll have those rascals toasty as marshmallows before you know it!"

September's hands and feet felt hot as she drifted off. They swelled white in her dream like marshmallows, then turned black and burst into flames. Gabrielle Barron laughed politely and beckoned her party guests away with a bell around her neck.

Bong bong bong.

"Come around now, you old cow!" Harry cursed his boat from above, and September woke with a start as she slid sideways in the bunk.

"Hard over!" she heard her dad calling from somewhere out on deck. The diesel engine reached a higher, more urgent pitch.

The bunk slanted the other way, and she bonked heads with a silent Ivan, who now showed a fresh bandage over his cut. Twice more they teetered, then the bunk found level and stayed that way. The screaming diesel slowed to a roar, then a gargle, and then the friendly *blump-blump-blump* of a relieved idle.

"Home sweet cove!" Harry said.

"I'll get Temmy. You bring Ivan." Her dad's voice sounded closer.

"Is that ol' Berger standin' on your dock?"

A groan. "I can't deal with him right now."

There was the sound of feet on the deck, and then a clunk of the gearbox and the propeller reversing.

"Berger!" her dad called from outside. "I got no time for your troubles. Grab this line."

"You got plentya troubles, Crane." Mr. Berger's mean voice replaced the sound of the engine. "I seen ya turn around the first time through my eyeglass. Then I seen the flare and the whole darn mess of it. Way I figure things, you got two half-drowned kids on board."

"Just tie that off and stand clear." Her dad's voice close again.

She felt hands slide beneath her.

"We're here," he whispered, pulling her face into his chest as he carried her up to the deck. She squinted into the clearing sky and saw the dummy hanging broad-shouldered and slack from the rigging. The smell of her dad's wet clothes had the same familiar scent as the dummy's, only she was the rag doll this time. Her dad stepped onto the dock and waited a moment. She could feel his trembling.

Harry came on deck with Ivan draped across his big mitts. "C'mon, Captain. Let's get off this old tub."

Her dad loped up the dock. "Berger, make yourself useful and get us a fire in that cabin."

September opened her eyes and saw the old man's pinched face moving right beside them, studying her.

"What do ya think I been doin'?" he said.

She and her dad looked up to the cabin and saw the hot smoke pouring from the chimney. When she turned back to Mr. Berger his expression did not seem as pinched or as mean. Mostly he looked like everybody else—tired and scared.

"I figured what happened, an' I rowed over here fast as I could." He turned a clouded eye to September. "I knew if ya got 'em back, this is the shape they'd be in. Seen it before."

"Thank you, Berger," her dad said. "And I apologize."

"No worry." Berger stepped off the path and gave way for Harry and her dad to charge the last steps to the porch.

The bear boards still covered the windows, and a single

186

kerosene lamp filled the cabin with a syrupy light. The gush of air when they pushed through the door nearly swooned them with its powerful warmth. A kettle and two other pots filled with heating water creaked and rattled on the blazing stove. A row of jars lined the shelf above, and a pile of towels lay beside the bed. Her dad stuffed September straight into the bed nearest the stove, and Harry dropped Ivan right beside her. The damp boat blankets were stripped away and replaced with their own soft quilts.

Mr. Berger stood bent in the doorway. Harry started dipping canning jars full of warm water from the pots and handing them to her dad. He screwed the lids on tight, wrapped them in towels, and stuck each one under the blankets into every nook and cranny of their fish-cold bodies. They felt like hot torches. Even Ivan complained from his distant planet with some garbled oath.

"Now we're cookin'!" Harry said as September watched the lamp on the table spin off into the distance with the shadow of Mr. Berger.

"United States Coast Guard, Bag Bay, Alaska. Over and out."

"Thank you, Lieutenant Mayhee. We're WBN6408 Steamer Cove, clear."

Voices and the smell of rose-hip tea filled Ivan's first waking thoughts. A tender light danced above him.

"Mom?" he said. No one.

A warm hand eventually came to his cheek. "It's Dad."

"Dad," Ivan said, trying it out, coming around. "Sep!" he cried, jerking to life. His face ached, and opening his swollen eyes felt like rolling logs off his head.

"She's here." His dad caught Ivan's groping hand and placed it on the mound of quilts beside him. "She's right here."

September twisted into a long, drowsy stretch.

"What time is it?" she yawned.

"You've slept for hours," her father said, reaching over to smooth her hair.

She looked around the dim room. The sorry episode started coming back to her in pieces. Two mugs sat on the table. "Is Harry here?"

"He's seeing Berger over to his place in the *Aunt Nelda*. The williwaw blew his dory home without him."

"Mr. Berger was here?" she asked, alarmed, then remembered. "He did a nice thing today, didn't he?"

Her father nodded wearily. "He probably saved your lives. He looked after you pretty well these last few days. A lot of people did."

Ivan was looking around the cabin, lost in the deep shadows of the oil lamp. "Who were you talking to just now?"

"The Coast Guard. Half the boats in the harbor were out looking for you. They found the skiff washed up on the mud flat in Huckleberry Cove—lucky for the *Four-O-Five*." Their dad didn't make it sound lucky.

"We made a mess of everything, didn't we?" September asked, feeling the troubles like the ache in her bruised chest.

"I'd say about everything, yeah." Their dad held up a mug of warm tea with honey for each of them to sip. "I'm too tired to be angry about this today," he said. "But I'll get around to it."

"I'm so sorry, Dad," September said. "I can explain how it all happened."

"Harry and Mr. Berger already told me *how*. What I can't imagine is *why* it happened." Her father took a sip of tea for himself and passed it to Ivan, who needed help tipping it. "You should have gone straight to Nelda's when you shorted the radios."

"I know," September said. "But we wanted you to trust us over here."

"I *did* trust you over here."

September noted the past tense. Ivan finally noticed something else.

"Hey, how did you talk to the Coast Guard without the radio?" he asked.

Mr. Crane managed a disbelieving smile. "That's the only thing that finally went right with your whole adventure. Harry found the radios jammed down the sleeves of that empty scarecrow thing left hanging in his rigging."

"The radios are working?" Ivan tried to sit up but winced with pain and lay back again with the help of his dad's hand.

"Easy there. You're banged up head to toe," his dad said. "And yes, after nearly drowning yourselves, Harry, me, and mobilizing half the boats in Bag Bay harbor in the worst blow of the year, the radios were still wrapped tight and work good as new. Not a mark on them. It's a good thing too. Harry lost his antennas, and his own radio gear got wet when the pilothouse blew open. We had no other way to let the harbor master and Coast Guard know we were all safe."

"How is the *Williwaw?*" Ivan asked innocently, remembering nothing of their rescue.

Mr. Crane turned to the sound of steps on the path outside. "Bad, but nothing that can't be fixed, and it's our responsibility to make it right with Harry. I'm afraid it's going to set us back on building the *Mrs Crane*."

Before Ivan or September could react to this terrible news, Harry opened the door. His huge shape hunched down as if he would sneak quietly in, until he saw them awake in the bed. "Well, look who's up! Hullo, Captain. G'd evenin', Little Miss."

"Hi, Harry."

"Hi, Hairy."

The big skipper leaned over with his hands on his knees to get a closer look at Ivan's face. "Hoo-boy! Them's gonna be a fine pair a shiners!"

He turned to September and let his bristly grin fade a degree. "Ya give your ol' pal Harry quite a scare out there today!"

She smiled up weakly from her pillow. "I'm sorry about your boat."

"Sorry about my boat!" Harry said. "Don't ya be sorry about the *Williwaw*! She had a terrific day! She's a little wet an' broke in spots, but she knows who she is now, by gosh! She knows who she is!"

September glanced at her father and away again. "I suppose we all do," she said.

Her dad sat heavily in his chair and looked from one to the other of them. A tense silence rang in the space around him.

Harry coughed and headed for the door. "By gosh, it's darker'n my boot in here! I think I'll go let some a this beautiful evenin' in."

Ivan and September watched their dad watching them. His jaw worked lumps into the side of his face and wobbled his temples. His mouth moved to say something—stopped—started again. He reached up and scratched the side of his head.

"It's my fault." He sighed. "I should have been home where I belonged."

"Me too," said September.

"And me," said Ivan.

Mr. Crane scratched his head another time, then stood. "Move over," he said.

They made way and sunk to the middle as their father's spent muscle and bone settled into the mattress between them. He dug an arm around their necks and lay with his eyes closed—breathing and listening to the sounds of the cove and Harry out fooling with the bear board on the window.

The loons spoke their hearts in a pair of bittersweet notes. There was the gentle trick-trickling of the tamed bay lapping at the dock piling—and a mysterious sound like wind on an open barrel.

"It's a killer whale in your cove!" Harry yelled, solving the mystery from the porch. "Swam right by an'—hoo! Lookit 'er blow!"

Ivan tried to rise and couldn't. September just listened, knowing she'd have to go outside to see it, and not able or willing to move. Their dad lay still, holding them.

"Not every day ya see that!" Harry called.

"Not in a lot of years," their dad finally said. "Must get driven in here by these storms. And they're called orcas—don't ever call them killers," he added gently and distantly.

He didn't open his eyes even when Harry pried the bear board loose and the cabin flooded with the ruddy reflections of the flame-colored sky. September took in the moody, beautiful light, and it landed on a big empty place inside of her.

"Do you think you'll ever trust us again?" she asked.

Mr. Crane let three long breaths come and go, then said, "Yes. But you'll have to earn it."

"How many clams does that cost?" Ivan remarked, hoping for a laugh that didn't come.

"Ivan." Mr. Crane heaved another breath. "Tomorrow I'm going to be rested, and I'm going to want to hear all about what was going through your head when you fooled with the radios like I told you not to."

"Yes, sir," Ivan said glumly, then thought of one more thing. "How did you ever know I was doing that in the first place?"

"That's a very good telescope our neighbor has over there," his father said, and gathered them each in a little closer. "But I'm not interested in what Berger sees right now. Ivan"—his father spoke from a place very near sleep—"I think it's your turn. Tell me what you see out there."

Ivan tilted his pounding head to the scene outside. The orca blew three white puffs across the cove. Mr. Berger's dim light reflected like a crazy laser in the whale-rippled water, and nothing looked as good to Ivan on either side of Bag Bay for as far as he could see.

"Red sky at night," he said, and waited for his sister.

"Sailors delight," she finished, and for the first time ever, there was no argument.

TOM BODETT is a storyteller recognized for his warm, humorous style, but he is perhaps best known as the spokesperson for Motel 6. He made his national broadcasting debut in 1984 as a commentator for National Public Radio's *All Things Considered*; he's currently the host of *The Looseleaf Book Company*, a national radio program about children's literature, and of the PBS/Travel Channel co-production *Travels on America's Historic Trails with Tom Bodett*, which has received two Emmy nominations. He is the author of many books and has recorded more than fifteen audiocassettes.

He lives with his family in Alaska.

THE VOYAGE OF THE <u>FROG</u>
by Gary Paulsen
0-440-40364-2

Fourteen-year-old David Alspeth intended only to fulfill his uncle's last wish when he set sail in the *Frog*, but when a savage storm slams the tiny sailboat, David is stranded. No wind. No radio. Little water. Seven cans of food. And the storm is just the first challenge David must face. . . .

An ALA Best Book for Young Adults

A *School Library Journal* Best Book of the Year

★"Paulsen gives readers another wonderful survival story. . . . Readers will have a real sense of participation and will be left hungry for more. . . . Hard to put down."
—*School Library Journal*, Starred

Available now from Dell Yearling Books

WHITE WATER
by PJ Petersen
0-440-41552-7

No way is Greg in the mood for white-water rafting with his father and his half brother, James. Greg's father thinks this expedition will make him more adventurous and help him get over his fears. But the trip becomes a nightmare when a rattlesnake bites Greg's father. There's no help nearby. Greg must take charge of the raft and, with James, get it through the rapids. Every moment counts. They must save their father's life.

An ALA Quick Pick for Young Adults

"The book is a thrill ride." —*Kirkus Reviews*

Available now from Dell Yearling Books